A Candlelight Ecstasy Romance®

KRYSTAL FELT THE HEAT RADIATING FROM HIS HAND TUCKED UNDER HER HAIR AT THE BASE OF HER NECK. . . .

"I don't break easily," she promised. "I'm very durable. Real crystal is made of sand and fire."

"Is that you, Krystal? Sand and fire?" His lips were very close to hers again. "You are very soft . . . and blond . . . and exquisite. *La joya . . . mi joya navidad . . . Christmas jewel.*" His hand slid under her short ski jacket.

"Like a rock . . ." she began. But her words were lost as his lips closed tenderly over hers. They moved possessively, ardently, with the stirrings of desire . . .

A CANDLELIGHT ECSTASY ROMANCE ®

154 A SEASON FOR LOVE, *Heather Graham*
155 LOVING ADVERSARIES, *Eileen Bryan*
156 KISS THE TEARS AWAY, *Anna Hudson*
157 WILDFIRE, *Cathie Linz*
158 DESIRE AND CONQUER, *Diane Dunaway*
159 A FLIGHT OF SPLENDOR, *Joellyn Carroll*
160 FOOL'S PARADISE, *Linda Vail*
161 A DANGEROUS HAVEN, *Shirley Hart*
162 VIDEO VIXEN, *Elaine Raco Chase*
163 BRIAN'S CAPTIVE, *Alexis Hill Jordan*
164 ILLUSIVE LOVER, *Jo Calloway*
165 A PASSIONATE VENTURE, *Julia Howard*
166 NO PROMISE GIVEN, *Donna Kimel Vitek*
167 BENEATH THE WILLOW TREE, *Emma Bennett*
168 CHAMPAGNE FLIGHT, *Prudence Martin*
169 INTERLUDE OF LOVE, *Beverly Sommers*
170 PROMISES IN THE NIGHT, *Jackie Black*
171 HOLD LOVE TIGHTLY, *Megan Lane*
172 ENDURING LOVE, *Tate McKenna*
173 RESTLESS WIND, *Margaret Dobson*
174 TEMPESTUOUS CHALLENGE, *Eleanor Woods*
175 TENDER TORMENT, *Harper McBride*
176 PASSIONATE DECEIVER, *Barbara Andrews*
177 QUIET WALKS THE TIGER, *Heather Graham*
178 A SUMMER'S EMBRACE, *Cathie Linz*
179 DESERT SPLENDOR, *Samantha Hughes*
180 LOST WITHOUT LOVE, *Elizabeth Raffel*
181 A TEMPTING STRANGER, *Lori Copeland*
182 DELICATE BALANCE, *Emily Elliott*
183 A NIGHT TO REMEMBER, *Shirley Hart*
184 DARK SURRENDER, *Diana Blayne*
185 TURN BACK THE DAWN, *Nell Kincaid*
186 GEMSTONE, *Bonnie Drake*
187 A TIME TO LOVE, *Jackie Black*
188 WINDSONG, *Jo Calloway*
189 LOVE'S MADNESS, *Sheila Paulos*
190 DESTINY'S TOUCH, *Dorothy Ann Bernard*
191 NO OTHER LOVE, *Alyssa Morgan*
192 THE DEDICATED MAN, *Lass Small*
193 MEMORY AND DESIRE, *Eileen Bryan*

DARING PROPOSAL

Tate McKenna

A CANDLELIGHT ECSTASY ROMANCE ®

Published by
Dell Publishing Co., Inc.
1 Dag Hammarskjold Plaza
New York, New York 10017

ISBN: 0-440-11657-0

Printed in the United States of America
First printing—December 1983

To Parris,
for friendship and high adventures
in New Mexico

To Our Readers:

We have been delighted with your enthusiastic response to Candlelight Ecstasy Romances®, and we thank you for the interest you have shown in this exciting series.

In the upcoming months we will continue to present the distinctive sensuous love stories you have come to expect only from Ecstasy. We look forward to bringing you many more books from your favorite authors and also the very finest work from new authors of contemporary romantic fiction.

As always, we are striving to present the unique, absorbing love stories that you enjoy most—books that are more than ordinary romance.

Your suggestions and comments are always welcome. Please write to us at the address below.

Sincerely,

The Editors
Candlelight Romances
1 Dag Hammarskjold Plaza
New York, New York 10017

CHAPTER ONE

Their eyes met across the crowded, smoke-filled lodge, and electricity sparked instantly. Questions were asked and replies given in that brief male-female exchange. He was clearly interested. She was definitely . . . curious.

Krystal had figured she was treading thin ice to attempt something so daring as crashing the party. The minute he started manuevering across the room, she knew she had made a mistake. He didn't take his eyes off her. It was obvious where he was headed. Oh, God—why did she come? Why did she listen to Jason?

Faking a nonchalant attitude, Krystal turned her attention to the small circle of amiable strangers. She stood on the perimeter, listening and nodding appropriately. They were a boisterous group, laughing heartily and clapping each other on the back. They accepted her as one of them. Perhaps they were too inebriated to notice that she wasn't.

Then he was beside her, his hand steadily under her elbow, steering her away from them. "Excuse me. Could we talk?"

She regarded the man, fully expecting him to escort her to the door. After all, she really didn't belong here, and he knew it. She could tell by the cognizant glint in his eyes. Those eyes! From a distance they were dark, perhaps gray. But up close they were a deep blue, and she was drowning in their depths. Momentarily she was swirled, whirled away, and Krystal felt as though she had known him forever . . . known him intimately. Those eyes alone seemed to capture her!

He smiled, as if he knew what she was thinking, and Krystal willed her mind to function alertly and her body to obey.

His voice caressed her like deep velvet. "Do you believe in magic?" He was standing very close, his hand still cupping her elbow, his arm against hers.

"No, not really." She breathed a little shakily. What was the worst he could do? Embarrass her publicly? Toss her out into the snow? Have his henchmen do the job for him? Surely he would just ask her to get the hell out, and she would, ruining her plans for the future. *Their* future. She took a quick breath, and his distinctive, masculine aroma filled her nostrils.

"This magic?" His long finger stroked the top of her hand, and tiny muscles quivered along her arm. "There is an irresistible attraction between us; surely you feel it. The minute I saw you, with that blond hair and those devilish green eyes, I knew. You are very enticing." His daring eyes lingered over her, caressing silently as his finger had done.

She had not expected *this,* so soon at least, and she answered with a little laugh. "Magic? It's the lights. And the festive season."

He smiled a little, enjoying their game. "Oh, no, it's not the lights. You're the one who has me dazzled. Are you here with anyone?" He looked around warily, as if expecting someone to sidle up.

"I came alone."

His grin was slightly crooked, and Krystal melted a little inside. Oh! He was handsome! It *was* magic! And this man was the sorcerer.

"I'm glad you did. I'm Gabe Marcos. And you?" He leaned slightly forward to catch her name, and the whisper of his aftershave invaded her senses.

"My name is Krystal."

"Krystal . . ." He repeated her name as if caressing it. "*Qué bonita.* It suits you. I must admit I'm curious about why such a lovely lady is here—alone."

Krystal answered more honestly than she cared to admit. "I—I was lonely. They say the holidays do that to people. A friend said it would be all right for me to come, though I wasn't invited. Is it?" Her tone was almost apologetic, and those emerald eyes appealed to him in such a way that he could never have told her no.

"Certainly you're welcome here! I'm glad you found us. I can't think of anyone I'd rather have crashing my party! I wouldn't want you to be lonely tonight."

Krystal shook her head, and her golden hair shimmered in the muted evening lights. "You're very kind, Gabe. And it's a lovely party, but I think it's time I was leaving." Suddenly she was afraid of what might happen if she stayed one minute longer.

Gabe pursed his lips. "It's much too soon to leave. Now that you're here, please stay. I'll see that you won't be lonely. More punch?"

Please stay? That was exactly what she wanted to hear. Or was it? Krystal shook her head in answer to his question, her sleek blond strands catching golden highlights from the multitude of candles providing the lighting in the room. "No, thank you. The punch is too sweet for me."

He glanced down at the half-full plastic glass in her hand. "It is, isn't it? Let me see what I can find. Excuse me for a minute. I'll be right back."

He took the glass and moved away, taking the aura of

magic, as he called it, with him. The man had left her with a warm glow inside, accompanied by a million butterflies. Krystal watched him disappear behind a rear door and breathed a sigh through her teeth.

So *that* was Gabe Marcos! He certainly was everything she had heard about him—and more. He had social finesse and was appealing in a rugged sort of way. Handsome, even. She would have to be aware of those pitfalls. After all, she had been warned and was going into this with both eyes wide open.

Moments later he was there, half-full wine bottle in one hand, two glasses in the other. As he gave her a crystal glass filled with white wine, their hands met. He had a warm, soothing touch, and Krystal marveled that he was so suave and sure of himself. And why did she feel like a thousand springs were bouncing inside her?

"This is all I could find. Shall we sit?" He motioned and steered her at the same time. There wasn't a chance to refuse.

"So are you in the mountains to enjoy some skiing? Where do you live?"

Krystal studied her glass for a moment and decided to answer the latter question and hedge on the former. "I'm from Albuquerque. But I love these mountains this time of year. They look like an old-fashioned Christmas card, with snow everywhere. And the villages are so quaint, with their *ristra* wreaths and *luminarias*. There is a unique beauty up here at Christmastime."

He nodded. "Christmas is an important time for the people who live around here. We try to make it special for the guests here at Starfire, too. In fact, later tonight there will be a torch procession off the mountain. Have you ever seen one?"

"Just once, several years ago." Did she dare reveal that the one holiday she had spent skiing had resulted in a broken tibia, and she had watched the fiery procession in misery with a fresh cast on her leg?

"Well, I'd like to show you a spectacular one tonight. We invite some of the villagers to join us, and they seem to enjoy it almost as much as we do. Frankly I think they like the parties they're invited to afterward."

Riotous laughter blared from the center of the room as if to prove his point. He waved toward the men. "You'll have to excuse the crew. They get a little rambunctious this time of year. You see, this is more than a Christmas party. It's also our anniversary."

"Anniversary?" Surely he wasn't married! She had been told he was a confirmed bachelor.

"Ten years." He nodded. "Ten years ago this Christmas we opened for business. Some of the original crew are still with me. Chris, there, is from France. Andrew, the director of the ski school, came here from Germany. Miguel is from Spain and in charge of the restaurants. He fixes an out-of-this-world paella! We even have a few Texas converts. Austin runs maintenance and grounds. His wife, Rita, heads our emergency services."

"You have a regular United Nations crew here. And a woman in charge of your paramedics! I must admit I'm impressed."

"Sure. She's a crackerjack, too. Had to drop out of medical school because of finances. We were lucky to get her. She takes care of any medical problems we have. Of course, skiing accidents are our most common." He turned back to Krystal and slid his hand sensuously over her wrist. It felt warm and steady, not nervous and icy, like hers.

"Do you have many? Uh, accidents?"

He shrugged. "The usual, I suppose. On TV, skiing looks easy, and people come up here ill prepared, thinking they can zip down the mountains without taking lessons. Most of our injuries happen because the individual is in poor physical condition."

Krystal smiled at the man across from her and tried to control her pulse. They were only exchanging small talk, but who was doing the manipulating here? She was exactly where she had hoped to be, planned to be—alone with Gabe Marcos. It was why she had come tonight. And yet there was this damned attraction, a magic between them, that she hadn't planned on.

At that moment they were interrupted by a man with a German accent. "Gabe, my boy, are you going to join us with the torches?" He clapped Gabe on the back and peered at Krystal across the table. "And who is this lovely fräulein?"

"This is my friend Krystal. Krystal, this is Andrew."

Andrew took her hand and brought it to his lips. "Entirely my pleasure, Krystal."

"Andrew, don't you think you should have a cup of coffee before you try to break your neck on that mountain?" Gabe suggested candidly.

Andrew obviously enjoyed skiing and beer with equal gusto. His response to Gabe professed his self-assurance. "Oh, hell! I'm steady as a rock! Are you coming along?"

"Not tonight. Pulled a hamstring. I'm getting too old for that sort of folly. Krystal and I will be watching from the main roof."

"Sorry, Gabe, you'll be missing great fun! Well, I'd better head out. So nice to meet you, Krystal." Andrew clapped Gabe on the back goodheartedly and tipped an imaginary hat to Krystal.

"Be sure to get that coffee!" Gabe ordered.

Krystal leaned closer to Gabe. "If you usually go, don't let me stop you. Please go ahead. I don't have to be entertained."

"*Ah, contrare!* I much prefer entertaining you, Krystal. And actually I did pull a hamstring. Haven't skied for several weeks because of it. Anyway, I don't want to give you a chance to get away."

Krystal smiled, thinking that getting away from Gabe was the last thing in the world she wanted. The crowd had begun to clear out somewhat, and the background music was suddenly audible. Several couples pushed aside the tables and began to dance.

"Shall we?" Gabe asked. "It'll be awhile before they get to the top of the mountain and are ready for the run."

Krystal smiled her agreement and swung easily into his strong arms. With her nose hovering near his chin, she again caught his beguiling, masculine fragrance. It was refreshingly different, like fresh mountain herbs, and it occurred to Krystal that Gabe Marcos was decidedly different from any other man she had ever known. His looks, his staunch dignity made him distinctive. There was a certain serenity about his smooth assurance and the protective feeling of his arms around her. Proud. Enchanting. Don't forget his smoothness, she reminded herself. He does this all the time.

Discreetly Krystal advanced her hand along his shoulder, figuring he must be at least six feet one or two. Her head came a little above his shoulder, and she had to tilt back to look into his bewitching blue eyes. She tried to stay away from them, concentrating instead on his square jawline.

Gabe Marcos was lean and had an athletic quality about his movements. Competence, proficiency, even grace emanated from every masculine cell. However, when she was propelled against his body, a stronger force of distinct power radiated from him, and Krystal felt caught up in that energy. He was durable and unyielding; she could feel it. The almost tangible strength of the man came from his arms, hands, chest, everywhere she touched! Oh, God, she needed that strength right now! So she clung to him, grateful for the slow dance that allowed this closeness.

They danced quietly, and Krystal tried to control her wildly racing emotions. She concentrated on his appearance. He was more rugged than handsome, too arrogant to be considered congenial. And yet it was said he had a generous streak. Beneath that chest of steel beats a heart so gentle, she thought with amusement.

His hair was black, and the proud way he held his head reminded Krystal of a pen-and-ink drawing of an Apache chief she had seen once. Even Gabe's skin was tanned to the color of ginger. Given these dark traits, one would expect his eyes to be ebony. At the very least they should have flecks of brown. But no, they were blue—not a Paul Newman blue but a deep cobalt blue that suggested mystery; a remote blue that reminded her of the distant Mediterranean. Now whatever made her think of that? Krystal had never seen the Mediterranean; she had no idea of its color. But his eyes carried her away . . . far away . . .

"Basques . . ." She said the word aloud and startled herself. Embarrassed, she looked up into those intense, all-knowing blue eyes that were wreaking havoc with her senses tonight.

"What was that?" His voice rumbled between them.

"I—I'm sorry. I just . . . your eyes." Krystal felt absolutely ridiculous, sinking even deeper in her own mire.

He chuckled amiably, as if to dispel her discomfort. "You know New Mexican history, don't you?"

"A little." She nodded.

"My ancestors were from Spain. They were Basques. That's what you said, isn't it?"

"Yes," she admitted ruefully. "I didn't mean to embarrass you." Gabe couldn't help but realize, though, that she was the one with color in her cheeks.

Gabe shrugged. "I'm not embarrassed at all. I'm proud of it. My father was a sheepherder in these mountains and valleys. So was my grandfather, and his father. That was before skiing came into vogue. They probably would be appalled to see what has happened to the mountains today. But, frankly, I would have made a lousy sheepherder."

"No, it doesn't seem to be your style. Too boring."

"There are times, though, when the peace and quiet of the hills sound inviting. Things around here can get pretty hectic, especially at this time of year."

Krystal considered his statement. "But a person in your position can always escape whenever you want to, can't you?"

He shrugged again, causing muscles to flourish under her hand. "Sometimes." His answer was vague, and she could tell he was avoiding further discussion. He pulled her closer, pressing her breasts against his chest. "Is that what you're doing here? Escaping?" His voice rasped through her. "And alone!"

"Perhaps . . ." She smiled evasively. Damned if she would tell him her true intentions tonight. Now was definitely not the time. But did he suspect? Did those penetrating eyes of his have special powers to look into her mind? More magic?

His tone was warm. "Now why would an attractive lady like you be trying to escape? A man? Husband?" He was searching for more information about her, and Krystal could sense his curiosity.

She smiled with pleasure. This was just what she wanted: his undivided attention. "Don't worry, Gabe. There's no husband. I'm happily divorced and have been for four years. Actually there's no man in my life right now." Why did she admit that? Wouldn't it be better to keep him guessing? Damn! She was no good at these social games.

"Good," he murmured against her ear. "I don't have to worry about an angry lover!"

"Would you worry, anyway?" she asked boldly.

His laugh was guttural and spontaneous. "Husbands I avoid like the plague! But lovers don't worry me."

"I thought as much." Krystal had the distinct feeling he spoke the truth. This man was not one to be intimidated!

"Krystal, you haven't answered my question. Who—or what—are you running from?"

She looked into the depths of his eyes. "What makes you think I am?"

"I don't know. I just have a feeling . . ."

She took a deep breath and tried to sound convincing. "I'm here to relax during the holidays, to escape the bustle of city life here in the mountains. That's all."

"I'm glad you chose Starfire. I think you will be very comfortable here. We'll make sure of it."

"Me, too," she agreed quietly, realizing that he thought

she was a patron of his ski lodge. In that moment Krystal wished she *were* there for a fling. Instantly an inner warning reminded her of her mission. Yet she enjoyed the feeling of Gabe Marcos's arms around her.

The dance ended and, reluctantly, they tore apart. Sitting at the little corner table, they finished their wine and exchanged tidbits of information about each other. They were enthralled by the magic that had drawn them together in the beginning and held them there all evening.

A clamor near the door brought their attention back to the Christmas party. "They're heading outside to watch the torchbearers," Gabe explained, and added with a flourish, "*Señorita,* would you like to accompany me to the most choice spot for viewing this spectacular event?"

"Why, yes, *señor,* I would love it!" Krystal smiled grandly and took his arm. They donned ski jackets and crunched through the snow to a blue Bronco.

"It's not far, but this will get us there quicker," he said as they got into the four-wheel-drive vehicle. He drove past the low buildings of the main lodge and parked in back, then led her up some lonely stairs. They climbed to a decked roof that afforded them a perfect view of the ski trails on the mountain that rose majestically behind them.

"I can see them gathering at the top!" Krystal cried excitedly, pointing to the flashes of lights hovering near the white peak.

"Ah, yes! Here they come! What a sight!" He exhaled enthusiastically.

"You're usually with them, aren't you, Gabe?"

"I'm usually at the head of the line!" he admitted. "But tonight I'm right where I want to be. Where I should be. For some reason I feel that both of us are in the right place." He moved closer, tucking her cold hand into the warmth of his pocket.

"Is that feeling part of the magic?" she whispered on a frosty breath.

"This is the magic . . ." His lips touched hers like silk, sending warm tingles through her veins. "Krystal, are you as delicate as your name? It sounds so fragile, as though you would break easily." Small kisses punctuated his observations. "And you look like what your name implies—fair and exquisite and sparkling." His other hand buried in her long golden mane.

Krystal felt the heat radiating from his hand tucked under her hair at the base of her neck. "I don't break easily," she promised. "I'm very durable. Real crystal is made of sand and fire."

"Is that you, Krystal? Sand and fire?" His lips were very close to hers again. "*La joya . . . mi joya navidad* . . . Christmas jewel . . ."

"Like a rock—" Her words were lost as his lips closed over hers tenderly. They moved possessively, ardently, warm with the beginnings of desire.

"You're very soft, Krystal, so soft . . ." His hand slid under her short ski jacket to lock around her ribs.

The magic moment was broken by loud cheers and shouts from below them. The first torchbearers were approaching, their long trail of fire zigzagging all the way up the snowy mountain. Gabe and Krystal watched silently, arm in arm, sharing the beauty. It only added to the enchantment of the night.

"Gabe, it's just beautiful," Krystal finally said with a sigh. "I've never seen anything so lovely!"

"I remember the first time I ever saw a torchlight procession. I was only six and—" Abruptly he halted.

"Yes? Go on, Gabe," Krystal encouraged.

His voice was gruff, and he turned his head away from her. "I don't know what made me say that. You aren't interested in what happened when I was six."

"I am, Gabe," Krystal assured him. She reached for his face, turning the square-jawed countenance toward her. "I am interested. Please continue."

The color in Gabe's blue eyes seemed to deepen. Apparently convinced of her sincerity, he began. "I was quite young when my father took me to see my first Indian ceremony. They didn't ski, of course. It was a religious event of celebration and thanksgiving. As they marched down from the mountaintop with lit candles, the sight of them was almost like ghosts of the past, resurrected for the night. It was beautiful . . . and eerie. I have never forgotten it."

She smiled. "I can understand why it made such an impression. Some of the Indian ceremonies are spectacular."

Gabe responded gruffly. "I don't know why I told you about that. I've never said it to anyone. We've had these processions off that mountain for ten years and those memories have never surfaced."

"Maybe it's because you're usually in the procession and don't see the full picture of those skiers zigzagging like that."

"You seem to have pegged it, Krystal." Gabe tightened his lips, knowing that it was memories of his father that he avoided, not the procession.

Afterward Gabe drove them away from the main buildings of the lodge, up a narrow road to a small cabin nestled against the side of the mountain. "How about a nightcap?"

Krystal looked at the small, lonely cabin. She knew the risks involved. They would obviously be alone, and she hardly knew this man. She knew *about* him, but there was a difference. Turning back to Gabe, she answered stiffly, "This is not why I came up here, Gabe."

"I know. A little coffee, then," he urged smoothly. "Later we can rejoin the party if you want to. It'll be going late into the night."

Krystal knew the party was not where she wanted to be. She wanted to be right here with Gabe Marcos! She smiled a faint consent. "All right, coffee." She put her hand on the door handle, and by the time she had climbed out of the Bronco, Gabe was there to assist her along the crunchy, snow-covered walkway to the cabin. A small, singular light radiated invitingly from inside a window.

They entered a large central room that included two sofas and several cushioned chairs gathered near a black, unlit fireplace. The kitchen and a small table adjoined the living room, and another door led to what was obviously a bedroom. The place was masculine and replete with Southwestern decor of tawny earth colors.

Gabe went first to the dark fireplace. Krystal watched his broad back as he bent to the task of starting a fire. When it flamed to his satisfaction, he went into the kitchen to make the coffee. The room was chilled, and Krystal stood in front of the blazing fireplace, warming her hands.

They were quiet until Gabe asked from the other room, "Have you been skiing yet, Krystal?"

"No. I'm waiting for more snow. I hear there are some dry patches."

"You're right. It's not entirely safe. But we should have snow by the weekend."

Krystal joined him in the kitchen, inhaling the satisfying fragrance of brewing coffee. "I suppose you look forward to the white stuff up here in the mountains, don't you?"

"We do snow dances on a regular basis around here—it's our bread and butter! Without snow, we don't exist!" He chuckled, and small brown crinkles spread from the corners of his blue eyes. Oh God, she was sinking again. Gabe mixed something in the coffee, topped it with a plop of whipped cream and handed it to her.

"What's this?" She peered curiously into the steaming cup.

"Just a little Irish coffee. That should help to warm you up. Why don't we go in and enjoy the fire?"

She sipped and raised her head with a smile. "Mmm, this is delicious!"

"This drink, plus the fire, should warm us sufficiently." Gabe settled another small log on the flames, then motioned for her to join him on the sofa. "You came up here to relax, Krystal. I'm here to see that you do. After freezing us both for an hour to watch the procession, the least I can do is thaw you out!" He laughed with satisfaction as Krystal sat on the sofa near his outstretched arm.

With a flowing motion that arm encircled her shoulders, pulling her close. Perhaps it was the enchantment they shared; it could have been the lure of masculinity that Gabe Marcos exuded. Or was it her own emotional weakness on this particular night? Krystal found herself leaning willingly against his chest, sipping her coffee contentedly beneath the weight of his arm, relaxing in front of Gabe Marcos's fireplace. It seemed so right that she should be there.

Krystal readily accepted his hypnotic kisses. Gabe's lips molded themselves lightly to hers, playing for a few moments with feathery brushes over her flushed skin. His velvet lips moved over her upturned face to kiss her forehead, eyelids, the lower edge of her jawline, then back to her lips, seeking the response he found. Her soft lips opened readily for his warm, thrusting tongue. Pushing his sweetly flavored tongue past her lips, he edged her teeth before exploring further. In eager anticipation she met him with her own stimulating tongue, inviting him deeper.

Flames of desire kindled within her as Gabe explored leisurely, easing Krystal into the curve of his strong arm. She stretched her arms around his neck, lacing her fingers in his jet black hair. His fragrance overwhelmed her in a heady mist, and she swirled with delightful abandon at his touch. It was a while before she realized that his tongue wasn't doing the only exploration.

Krystal awakened to spiraling sensations as her breasts automatically responded to his warm touch. Beneath her sweater, his hand fondled the soft, feminine mounds. Small gasps of pleasure escaped her throat as her nipples drew into tight knots of desire.

"Oh, Gabe, we mustn't . . ." Krystal struggled half-heartedly. His kiss, his touch had sparked flames long dormant in her, and she hated to end this pleasure. But end it she must!

He allowed her to struggle until she realized that her wriggling only served to nestle her closer against his reclining body, effectively pinning her to the sofa beneath him. Again his hand slipped beneath her sweater to seek her heated, throbbing flesh. She longed for his touch, yet vaguely, in the recesses of her mind, she thought of the risks.

His knee wedged between hers, allowing room for his

hand to tease her thighs and upward until he reached her waist. "Relax, Krystal. Can't you feel how special this is? How special I think you are? There's no harm in what we're doing."

No harm? What would this do to their relationship? Would this ruin everything? Before Krystal had time to come to a reasonable conclusion, his knee thrust upward, pressing gently, and his hand again sought her breast.

He hovered above her, his teasing eyes looking deeply into hers. "Your body responds to me, Krystal, whether you want to admit it or not. You know what's happening." He tugged gently on each hard, rosy tip.

Krystal smiled in spite of herself. Damn him, anyway! Even though she was aware that this was too fast, too bold, she was enjoying every minute, and he knew it!

"Now that's what I like to see. A little joy in your somber face, Krystal. You're so pretty . . . *qué bonita.* We belong together tonight." He kissed her cheek and temple where a tiny damp curl coiled.

She smiled and nodded, the length of her hair fanned out on the sofa like golden threads. "It seems that way, Gabe. It's just . . ."

"Too soon, right?" he completed for her, shifting so he could look gently into her eyes.

"Yes," she admitted. "I don't usually—that is, I don't ever . . ."

"Krystal," he whispered, hushing her. "It's not too soon if it's right for both of us. And I believe this encounter was meant to be. It's right . . ."

His lips brushed her silken eyelids, then her finely textured cheek. She parted her pink lips, admitting his firm, probing tongue, but before she could capture it, he continued his maddening kisses down her chin and neck, setting her passion aflame, a wildfire licking over her entire body. When he reached the soft swell of her breasts, his kisses made fiery halos of delight over her sensitive skin, and she sighed pleasurably at the long-forgotten responses. His tongue encircled the luscious peaks, teasing each to ripe, eager prominence. She arched against his heated breath, responding beyond her wildest imagination to Gabe's sensual touch.

"Oh, Gabe . . ." It was a small whimper. Oh, how she wanted him!

"It's much more comfortable on the bed, Krystal," he murmured thickly, and with a flourish he swept her up in his arms and carried her through the adjoining door.

Krystal clung to his broad shoulders and kissed his warm neck as they moved together into the bedroom. He placed her on the bed and eased her sweater over her head. "Gabe—" she said. But there were no more protests as he bent down, paying dutiful homage to each creamy breast, now so beautifully revealed.

She reached for him, pulling his face closer to hers, tempting him with another kiss. She wanted to resist—and yet she didn't. She knew she should stop him while she still could. But something beyond her control held her captive in his arms. It had been so long—so long since she had responded to a man. This time seemed so right, for she found Gabe Marcos irresistible. She would worry about the problems this would create later. Now was the time for Gabe and her, just the two of them.

His sweater tickled her bare breasts, rubbing erotically over them before the crush of his chest covered them completely. His kiss was forceful, his tongue plundering maddeningly. While her hands locked unconsciously around his neck, his hands pushed on her woolen slacks.

In another few minutes Krystal was completely naked in his arms. He kissed her quickly, then moved away. As coolness waved over her heated body, she watched Gabe shed his clothes. His male form was lean and muscular and quite tanned all over.

She observed with curious fascination his well-formed arms and chest, each lacking the usual heavy mat of masculine hair. His body was quite smooth and inviting. His stomach was flat and revealed a spare line of dark hair that would normally be hidden from view. His hips were slim, with taut muscles merging into hard, sinewy thighs.

He turned to face her, and she marveled at his rigid form, knowing she should stop this, realizing she couldn't. Maybe she didn't even want to. If she was honest with herself, she wanted to feel his warm, firm body excitingly against her.

She opened her arms to Gabe, and he slid close to savor her delectability. His tongue created havoc with her senses, and tiny moans of ecstasy escaped her as he touched certain sensitive spots.

"Krystal . . ."

"Yes?"

"Has it been a long time for you?"

"Yes—how did you know?"

"It doesn't matter. It just makes this even more special for us. Like I knew it would be." He touched her softly.

She cradled his face in her hands and kissed his lips, murmuring, "Oh, yes, Gabe. It is special."

"I want you, Krystal," he moaned against her ear and pulled her impatiently against his firmness.

"Yes, I want you, too, Gabe."

"You are beautiful, Krystal." His large, dark hand admiringly traced her soft, feminine curves. He kissed her waiting lips while his exploring hand sought the hardened peaks of her breasts, teasing them between thumb and forefinger. Long fingers spread across her ribs, then moved to her flat belly and her tufted female mound of desire. She arched against his hand, telling him clearly that she wanted him now.

"Krystal, should I—are you—" Gabe hesitated, and Krystal suddenly understood what he was asking.

She shook her head, feeling shy and very naive.

"Don't worry, *mi amor,* I'll take care of everything." He rose from her and fumbled in a nearby drawer.

With deep embarrassment, she realized that her inexperience was showing. Krystal was grateful that one of them was thinking clearly. He was absolutely right. It had been a long time for her. And his touch set her on fire while forcing her to forget all reason.

When he rejoined her, she pulled him to her, eager to receive the heat of his aroused masculinity. She looked up to see him watching her lovingly and she knew the image of his dark, passionate face would linger in her memory forever. She closed her eyes, and the image was imprinted there, as if she had snapped a photograph inside her mind.

His eyes were full of joy as he watched her expression change to one of passionate satisfaction at the moment of their union. A small cry of joy escaped her smiling lips, and Krystal opened her eyes long enough to see the dark form descending to capture her lips as well as her entire yearning body. The wild sensations that flooded through her when he joined his body with hers were like none she had ever felt. Never before . . .

For a moment she thought—wished—the feelings would last forever. There was such a magnetic force between them that they both felt the electricity sparking in a singular, giant explosion that rocked the bed.

"Oh, Gabe," Krystal murmured as she relaxed beneath him. "I can't believe it. So good . . ."

With a sweep of his long arm he pulled the quilted coverlet over them both and cuddled her closely in his arms. "I know. It was magic, Krystal. Pure magic. We belong together."

And because she wanted to believe him, Krystal relaxed, sated, in Gabe's arms. They dozed while the cold New Mexico night closed in around them.

Sometime before dawn Krystal awoke and slipped noiselessly from the bed and Gabe's warm body. Before the dying embers of the fireplace she dressed hurriedly. She pulled on her boots, zipped up her ski jacket and quietly left the cabin. The early-morning air was bitter and cold but served to sober her. She hiked the distance back to the building complex and her car. It gave her time to reflect on the events of the night.

The decision to go to the party had probably been one of her more irrational ones. What had she thought she would do? Sit in the wings and observe Gabe Marcos from afar?

No, she had had him right where she wanted him: drinking a little wine and exchanging small talk. It had been fun. Watching the skiers? That had been beautiful. In fact, the evening had been perfect. Or had it?

A little nightcap? That was innocent enough, but before she knew it, they were together on the bed. Worse yet, she had been willing! Krystal couldn't believe she had been so foolish as to throw away the future for one night of ecstasy!

Damn! This is the dumbest thing I've ever done! Krystal fumed to herself as she unlocked the cold car. She knew she had to face him again.

Krystal watched her frosty breath for a few minutes while the motor warmed before driving off into the dawn.

CHAPTER TWO

"This is the bridal suite." The dark-haired bellhop smiled grandly and opened the heavy wooden door. Stepping aside, he motioned to her and said in a heavy Mexican accent, "Mr. Marcos will join you shortly."

"Thank you," Krystal murmured and walked into the room as if it were the most natural thing she had ever done. Actually it was the most presumptuous. Her self-esteem was at stake here, and her future. For a nervous, panicky moment she wondered what in the world she was doing.

What had made her think this would work? How could she approach him now? Could she possibly consider another meeting with this legendary kingpin of the mountain and come out unscathed? Was this another foolish move? Should she slip out before he arrived? No! She refused to give in to her self-doubts.

Krystal peered around the masterfully decorated bedroom. The dark woods of typical Southwestern design had been abandoned for brass and glass in the sitting area and bar, while a mirrored wall reflected the major emphasis of the two rooms: the bed. The graceful still life of deep-hued suede and satin piled high with additional pillows was definitely a sensuous focal point, conducive to romance. Was that why he had requested their meeting in this room?

On second thought, he probably didn't even know who

she was, other than a client who had made an appointment. She had carefully stated only her last name to the secretary when she called. She intended to meet him on nonpersonal terms today.

Thoughts of their night together flooded her mind embarrassingly. It had seemed right at the time, but now she couldn't be sure. It had been less than a week since that fateful night, and Krystal fervently wished she could have postponed this meeting. She wanted to give them both a chance to reconcile it as a frivolous fling—or forget it altogether. And yet Krystal knew that for her forgetting was impossible.

However, she was pressed and had no more time to lose. It was time to get down to business.

Walking to the spacious window, Krystal gazed out at the glittering silver landscape. As Gabe had predicted, the weekend had provided new snow that cloaked everything, casting a clean image on the world and bolstering the ski business. "Our bread and butter," he had said that night, and she knew it to be true. There was a possibility that the weather could also affect *her* future, if only . . .

She straightened her collar in the window's reflection, slightly nervous at the prospect of seeing Gabe Marcos again. What would he say when he saw her? Then an awful thought struck her. Would he remember?

Her question was answered soon enough.

A familiar velvet voice wrapped around her. "Ms. North? Sorry to keep you waiting. I see you've found our spectacular view."

Krystal turned to look into the mysterious blue eyes of the man who loomed in the doorway. He was taller than she recalled, and more intimidating. She sucked in her breath resolutely because, from the first, she had known this moment would come.

His eyes shimmered with fascinating lights as he recognized her. There were elements of surprise, relief, even warmth in their depths. *Oh yes,* his expression told her immediately. *He remembered!*

She smiled softly, suddenly overcome with a mixture of feelings ranging from embarrassment to joy at the sight of him.

Gabe stood speechless for a second. In the sunlight Krystal was even more attractive than she had been in flickering candlelight. Her hair was absolutely golden, and those emerald eyes were entrancing. Why had she been so elusive? He wanted to embrace her and castigate her both at the same time.

His mouth, the lips that had kissed her so passionately, formed a welcoming grin. His eyes, those never-to-be-forgotten depths of Mediterranean blue, caressed her brazenly. His hands, which had made the magic last late into the night, gestured impotently.

Gabe's first words were sharper than he had intended. "Krystal! What are you doing here? I've looked everywhere for you. Where have you been? You certainly weren't staying at the lodge."

She smiled shakily, feeling suddenly like a limp rag doll in his dynamic presence. How could she explain her strange behavior? It was with great effort that she started to speak. "No, I haven't been at Starfire, Gabe. After our—night together, I went back home."

"Home? Back to Albuquerque? Why didn't you stay?"

His words hung in the air, and Krystal groped to explain why she hadn't stayed.

The uncomfortable moment was interrupted by a white-uniformed, dark-haired woman who wheeled a small food cart into the room. "In here, Mr. Marcos?"

"Just leave it there, *gracias,* Delores. That's all." He dismissed the woman impatiently, then turned a wry smile to Krystal. "I must admit I didn't expect you. You never even told me your last name. I thought you were here to schedule a convention or plan a skiing package for a group you represented."

"Is that why you're entertaining me in the bridal suite?" she mused.

He gestured toward the window. "Frankly, yes. The view is better from this room than from my office." He moved across the room and drew the drapes fully open. "If I'm trying to sell a package, I like to show off some of the best qualities of the lodge."

Krystal's eyes followed his direction, and she nodded. "Yes, I can see that logic. The view from here is spectacular. But you must admit the room is suggestive."

"I don't mean it to be. People who arrange conventions usually want to see what the rooms look like."

"Obviously that's not why I'm here, Gabe."

"No, I assumed as much, Krystal." He moved to the sofa, leaning casually against it and folding his long arms across the chest on which she had once nestled. "Would you like to sit?"

She shook her head, then instantly regretted it, thinking her legs might not hold her sufficiently. "I—first I want to apologize for my behavior the night we met. It's not like me to—to—"

"Spend the night?" he supplied with slight amusement at her discomfiture.

"Yes! I have never been so—so impulsive! I shouldn't have stayed."

"Don't apologize for something so natural, Krystal. I don't regret one moment we spent together. I'm sorry you do."

"It was too fast . . ."

"It was special. You even said so, Krystal."

"Maybe I was mistaken," Krystal tried weakly.

Gabe stood and took a step, halting so close to her she feared he could hear her heart pounding. One large hand cupped her jaw fiercely. "It was no mistake, Krystal, and you know it." His lips descended on hers with such force and speed that Krystal felt his teeth press painfully against her tender lips. There was none of the silky-soft persuasion of their previous encounter. This was a strong, insistent kiss, demanding a response.

And, oh God, did she sizzle inside at his touch! Just seeing him again was bad enough, but this kiss sent her reeling! She swayed weakly forward to meet his fierce approach, all the while trying to protest.

As quickly as it began, it was over. He broke their untamed contact and glared at her, his intense blue eyes searching for her reaction.

Although Krystal thought her knees would buckle with the weakness that raced through her, she struggled to maintain an indifferent facade. She dabbed at her throbbing lips with her fingertips. "Gabe, don't—" she said hoarsely in surprise. A shaky hand reached up to brush back a wanton strand of hair.

His hand automatically sought the loose wisp and pushed it back from her face, caressing her gently in the process. His voice mellowed. "I didn't mean to hurt you, Krystal. I just had to know if the magic was still here. I think it is. Why did you leave me that night? Running away again?"

She faltered and quivered involuntarily at his tender touch. "Please believe me when I say that I just couldn't stay. It really was a mistake, Gabe. I shouldn't have . . ." Her voice dwindled to a hoarse whisper.

"No, Krystal. You're wrong."

"I know—know my own feelings!" The minute she said it, she knew it was a lie. But it was the only way to create the emotional break she needed.

Gabe jerked his hand away from her with a growling sound. "Damnit, Krystal, you're not making any sense. None at all! I thought—"

"Well, you thought wrong!" she answered more snappily than she had intended. "Can we call what happened between us an unfortunate incident and put it aside?"

He sighed heavily. "I'm not sure I agree with you, but if that's what you want, I can accommodate." Gabe turned away from her and motioned toward a chair. "Please have a seat. I think we need to discuss a few things. Would you like some hot tea?" He moved to the little food cart.

Krystal sank weakly into the chair. She had to get a grasp on her emotions and overcome this traitorous trembling so she could get on with her business. After all, that was really why she had come.

Gabe leaned toward her and their hands touched, creating a spark of electrical magic as he handed her the steaming cup. "Do you like spiced tea?"

She smiled sheepishly, thinking it terribly embarrassing that they had spent the night together yet he didn't even know her drink preferences. "Yes, thank you."

Gabe folded his tall frame into the chair opposite her and sighed. "Look, Krystal, I can see that you regret everything about that night. But I'm convinced it was a special evening with lots of magic for *both* of us."

Her green eyes softened at his frank admission. "I didn't mean to imply that the evening wasn't wonderful, Gabe. Most of it was lovely. You were very gracious at the party, and the torch procession down the mountain was very beautiful. However, I just don't like the idea of going to bed with a man the first evening we meet." She shifted uncomfortably and crossed her long legs.

"Krystal, there was a spark between us that night. From the beginning, there was a magic. We simply responded to it, as adults will do. Today, though, all of that seems to be gone . . . at least for you." His eyes darkened at her rejection.

"No, it isn't all gone. It's just that now there are other things to consider." She could feel herself calming a bit. Perhaps it was because this endeavor was so important to her future.

"Like what?"

She took a deep breath. "I—I thought we could talk business."

"Business? It must be important for you to have driven all the way up from Albuquerque. That's twice in one week."

"Actually, Gabe, I didn't have to drive all the way from Albuquerque. I'm living closer."

"Oh? So you lied about that, too?"

She raised her eyes quickly to him. "Lied? No, I said I was from Albuquerque and I am. I just moved from there last month. Now I live near here."

His eyes narrowed. "Where?"

"The High Valley Ranch."

Gabe's head jerked around, a soft expletive escaping at

the same time. "You live in that art colony to the west of here?"

Her smile was tight but assured. He recognized the name. "The High Valley Ranch has changed owners. It's mine now."

"What?" He spat the word out with force.

Krystal nodded confidently now that she had his full, shocked attention. "Yes. The land came to me through an inheritance, and I decided to move my business here a few weeks ago."

Gabe's face clouded ominously for the first time that day. The picture was somewhat changed now. She was no longer a beautiful woman. She was an adversary! "I see," he reflected, tight lipped. "Then old Theo Reese has died, eh? No one told me."

"Should you have been notified?" Krystal sipped the last of her tea and set the cup aside. "Actually I hardly knew my uncle. As a matter of fact, when I was notified of his death and the huge inheritance of land, I was amazed. He never cared for material things, and the fact that he had an estate at all was a surprise to me."

Gabe watched her closely for a moment, then rose and paced before the window with the spectacular view. However, the scenery was far from his mind now. "Well, Krystal, are you going to continue in your uncle's footsteps and keep the art colony going? He was adamant about that, you know." There was a gruffness, perhaps a resentment in his tone that Krystal didn't fully understand.

"Oh, no." She smiled with satisfaction. "I intend to turn it into a health spa."

"A what?" Gabe's eyes widened as he returned to his position opposite her.

"A health spa. You know, there's a natural hot springs

on that property which has never been fully utilized," she explained.

"I know all about that land."

"Then you must know it's a perfect spot for such a business. And the timing is right." Krystal's enthusiasm grew as she discussed the possibilities. It represented her new life, her exciting new beginning—for the second time. And she was determined to make this one work.

"Well, I'm not so sure about the timing. And who wants a health spa up here in the mountains? People go to Phoenix for that!"

"I do. I want it right here. And I think others will, too!"

He shifted. "Uh, Krystal, before you make any big plans, let's discuss this business. I have some personal interest in that High Valley property."

She smiled confidently. "That's exactly what I hoped you would say, Gabe. Believe me, people would love to have a health spa up here in these mountains! Not everyone likes to ski, you know. The biggest advantage, though, is that tourists could come to the spa year-round, not just when it snows."

"My concern for that land is to, ah—retain its natural beauty, not to commercialize it by turning the place into a health spa, Krystal." He waved his hand in a tiny circle, indicating his notion that her ideas were crazy.

However, Krystal had expected his resistance, and she remained calm and smiling. "My plans would complement your commercial property—maybe even enhance it."

He leaned toward her and measured his words. "I don't know what you're after, Krystal, but I want to purchase that land. I've tried for years to buy it from your stubborn uncle, but he wouldn't sell. You probably know that already. Before you get your ideas and business off the ground, we should talk seriously about this. I will make it very profitable if you sell now."

"I'm sorry, Gabe. The property isn't for sale. That stubborn Reese has an equally stubborn niece."

Suddenly Gabe's voice softened to a soothing resonance. "Let's not make any rash decisions today, Krystal. Let my lawyer contact yours with a proposal."

She shook her head, and golden silk shimmered in a ray of sunlight. "No, Gabe. I've made an assessment of the place, and I like what I see. Furthermore, I've already moved to the ranch. I love it! The valley is beautiful, and I have decided to live and work there."

"Krystal, don't hem yourself into a helpless situation. There is no hope for a business such as yours up here. It's ski country and that's it!"

"Don't be so narrow-minded. Just because no one has a spa up here doesn't mean it won't catch on. Why, when people see the natural, unaltered beauty of the area and how the valley rises slowly to meet the mountains on either side—"

Gabe's words exploded to interrupt her description. "I know how the valley rises!" He clamped his jaw shut, leaving an ominous muscle jerking in his swarthy cheek.

Krystal observed his vehement reactions for a moment, then chose to make her move. It would obviously take a lot of persuading to change his obstinate mind, so she might as well start now, she thought.

She stood and walked slowly to the window, gazing out at the magnificent, snow-covered mountain. Turning back to him, Krystal stuffed her hands in her pants pockets. Pursing her lower lip slightly, she proposed, "I'd like to start discussing that business right now, Gabe. What would you say about a merger of your corporation and mine?"

The words seemed to freeze in the tense silence of the room as Gabe Marcos, undisputed king of the Sangre de Cristo Mountains ski resort, stared in astonishment at the brazen blond woman.

His sarcastic laughter filled the cold space between them. "Merger? You're crazy! Why would I even consider merging with you? I'm the one with the established business here. And I have no interest whatsoever in including a health spa in my organization. There's nothing in it for me."

Krystal approached him, her long legs emphasized by tapered pants and boots. "Oh yes, there is. For one thing, you wouldn't have to worry about running the spa. That would be my part of the business. However, it's a year-round proposition. You would share in those profits. We will certainly have more to offer in the summer than you presently do.

"Then there's that horrible winding mountain road that leads up here. How convenient it would be to cut a road easement through my property and directly up to Starfire. It would be easier for you to keep it clear of snow and in good driving condition. And it would definitely be safer than that hazardous donkey trail you use now. You could profit from a road cut through my property, Gabe."

"Your property—" he sputtered as the words fell bitterly from his lips.

Krystal raised her brows, and her emerald eyes met his steadily. "Of course. The off-season trade could be quite profitable. I'm moving my boutique to the valley. The luxury spa would accommodate those who don't care for skiing but still want some form of invigorating exercise.

"We'll have an equipment room, hot-springs spa, exercise programs, nutritional meals for weight loss and everything one needs for better health. The natural beauty of the land will provide the rest." She folded her arms, outwardly confident of the merits of her bold proposal, inwardly praying he would agree.

Gabe stood, the full six feet two inches of him towering above her. "I've been established in this ski resort for ten years and have never needed to offset my trade with a spa and boutique!"

"Don't you think it's time you branched out? You might consider it for access to a new road, if nothing else. It could work positively for both of us." Krystal fought a weakness that engulfed her as she stared defiantly into his dominant gaze.

"Now I see why you crashed my party," he said through his teeth. "And the seduction was your act, not mine!"

Krystal propped her fists angrily on her hips. "That's not so! How can you say such a thing? You were the one—"

The tight moment was pierced by the jangling of the phone. Gabe grabbed it, and Krystal turned an irate stare out the window.

His response was sharp and clipped. "Yes . . . yes, I'll be right there."

When he hung up the phone, there was a heavy silence in the room, and Krystal could feel his menacing eyes ripping through her. Finally she wheeled around and gathered up her ski jacket. "Well, it's been very interesting, Gabe. If you change your mind and decide you want to talk business, you know where to find me." She strode angrily to the door. "We're neighbors now, Gabe, whether you like it or not. And we can either work with each other or against each other. The choice is yours."

He glared at her, his angular face a tight, muscular structure. "I'll think about it. And be in touch."

She gave him a fetching smile. "Good. I'll look forward to our next business meeting." Krystal glided from the sumptuous honeymoon suite and down the deeply carpeted hall, sighing with relief, though she was still shaking inside from the encounter. She hadn't anticipated his kiss or her own uncontrolled reaction to it. Just what was he trying to prove? That he had some sort of power over her?

Perhaps he did. She had been unaware until the moment they touched in the cold light of day just how strongly the man affected her. What would that do to their relationship? Their *business* relationship? Could they ever discuss things like personnel and financial statements and accounts receivable? If they could only forget that night . . . but Krystal knew she couldn't. It was too special.

Now what? Well, for one thing, she would let Gabe Marcos make the next move. He had said he would think about it. Was there hope? How long would she have to wait? Would it be too long for her? Would he outwait her? She couldn't hold on to that property too long without his help. But then he didn't know that.

Krystal took the stairs two at a time and entered the lobby. She looked around with a different perspective this time. Was it possible that someday this would be hers—or partly hers? Was she being presumptuous? What made her think Gabe Marcos would ever come around to her way of thinking?

But there was something in his eyes; a flicker in those sensitive, beautiful eyes that told her he would call. Krystal stepped out into the blinding New Mexico sunlight, her footsteps crunching on the snow-covered lawn of Starfire Ski Resort. She dreaded the treacherous trip back down the mountain on that narrow, winding road.

Deep, brooding eyes watched her from the window above as Krystal opened the door to her compact car. She kicked the snow from her boots and slid behind the wheel. Her blond hair glistened in the sunlight, and his masculine senses responded with appreciation, just as they had that night. Oh yes, she had a way of intriguing him that was disconcerting. He wanted her again. Now! In spite of her disturbing announcements today.

Damn, he must be crazy. Krystal cared for nothing and no one. Hadn't her reactions shown him that? Then why did he let her disturb him so?

She didn't even care about that land. Not like he did, anyway. It was just a place to be, a location to start her business. But he had to have it. He had to put a stop to her plans.

I'll pay her damn well for it! he thought, clenching his large hands into fists. She has no strong ties to that land . . . my land. Surely I can persuade her, bring her around. He watched her car creep through the first hairpin curve on the narrow road that led down the mountain. Then he turned back to the dark-skinned man in his office.

"What do you mean, you're quitting? You have a job to do, Juan. There's a busload of tourists coming in this afternoon. You've only been working here nine months! The season's just getting started. Give it a little more time—*más tiempo, hombre!*" Gabe Marcos's expressive eyes glinted angrily as he shifted his thoughts to the problem before him.

The simply dressed man shuffled his feet and shifted his sombrero from one hand to the other. "No more time, *señor.* I'm going back home."

"You've tried that already and it didn't work. Now that we've gotten your green card, I can help make things happen for you. But you have to stay here in the States!"

More shuffling. "*Gracias, señor.* But my family needs me there."

"I told you we could bring them over, too. It just takes time." The two men stared silently at one another for a long minute. "I can't believe you're quitting, after all I've done for you, the risks I took—for you! I'm disappointed!"

"*Sí, señor.*" The man studied his shoes.

"Well, at least stay for the week. Give me time to find a replacement to drive that bus."

The man's dark eyes lifted in fear. "No, *señor.* No more driving the bus! That road! *Está el trabajo del diablo!* No more driving!" He started to back away.

Gabe's jaw stiffened. It wasn't the first time employees had quit or refused to drive the commuter bus down the treacherous mountain road. It just emphasized his compelling need for that valley property and a better access.

"Juan, you'll never make it in this world by quitting. Quitting isn't the answer! Hard work is! You have to—oh, hell. *Ve usted!* You don't know what I'm talking about, do you?" He motioned futilely with his large hand.

"*Gracias, señor.*" The man moved toward the door.

"*Uno mòmento,*" Gabe asserted as he scribbled something on a slip of paper. "*Aquí,* take this to the office. You can pick up your final check, *su dinero. Y buena suerte.*" Two bronze hands clasped briefly in mutual kinship.

"*Sí, señor. Gracias, gracias.*"

Gabe sighed heavily and watched almost sadly as the man shuffled from the elegant, wood-paneled office. His restless blue eyes paused momentarily on the familiar Starfire logo painted on rough-hewn wood and mounted on the wall near the door. It reminded Gabe of the years of hard work, the lonely days and nights, the deals he had made that finally propelled him into his present position of power in New Mexico.

He hadn't been an overnight success. And the money it took had been hard to come by. But he had done it. Now he could manuever people and situations the way he wanted them to go. Krystal would be no exception, he determined. But a niggling doubt stuck with him.

He couldn't get her out of his mind—Krystal, with the silky blond hair he could almost feel even now! He wanted her. But he also wanted that land. That was what he had worked for all his life. He would get it, too. It was just a matter of time.

Gabe Marcos turned to gaze out the window behind his desk as skiers criss-crossed the snow-covered mountain that loomed above them. His eyes settled on the simply dressed man who shuffled across Starfire's front lawn.

Gabe hunched his broad shoulders and stuffed his hands into his pockets. Years ago he had resolved to conquer whatever obstacles confronted him. This was a mere inconvenience. An employee who decided to quit was nothing compared to some of the management and personnel problems he faced almost daily.

There are ten men eager to replace Juan. Forget him, Gabe told himself. But there was something about the man—any man who quit. A small, raging fury grew inside Gabe as he considered the poor alternatives that would face Juan when he returned home. There was nothing if the man wasn't willing to sacrifice. But then not everyone was as willing to sacrifice—to work hard—to never quit—like Gabriel Marcos.

CHAPTER THREE

"Guess what, Krystal. An interesting thing happened late yesterday afternoon. I got a call from Gabe Marcos's lawyer. He's prepared to make an offer to buy your property! I did some checking, and it seems he's been relentlessly dogging your uncle for years, trying to purchase that land."

Krystal pushed a golden strand back from her eyes and murmured, "Is that right? So that's what he meant . . ."

The voice over the phone crackled with static. "What? I can't hear you, Krystal. Have you talked with him recently?"

She raised the timbre of her voice. "Yes, Jason. Matter of fact, I talked with Gabe Marcos just yesterday."

"Business?" Jason's voice sounded farther away than Albuquerque.

"Yes, of course."

"Did you mention the merger? Was he receptive? Come on, Krystal. Stop playing games! Why didn't you call earlier and warn me?"

"Warn you?" She was perturbed by Jason's attitude as well as by the actions of Gabe Marcos. "I had no reason to think you needed to be warned. I thought I made myself perfectly clear to Gabe Marcos yesterday."

Jason chuckled sarcastically. "Apparently the only

thing perfectly clear to Marcos is the fact that you now have some property that he thinks he can get."

"Damn!" Krystal muttered through her teeth.

"Did you two discuss the merger? Did he sound interested?"

Jason was as business-oriented as Gabe Marcos, she thought disgustedly. "Yes, I mentioned the merger. And no, he wasn't thrilled with the idea," she said harshly.

"Exactly what did he say, Krystal?"

She laughed sarcastically. "He'd be in touch."

"Well, hell! He was in touch, all right!"

"Now, Jason, how many times have you said those very words to a prospective client? I expected less, frankly. We must give Gabe time to consider it. Eventually we might even need to convince him that this merger is a good idea for him as well as for me." She sounded much more reassuring than she felt.

"Should I call his lawyer?" Jason was certainly eager to get this deal going.

Quickly Krystal discouraged the idea. "Oh, no! Not yet. Give me time, Jason."

"Time is one thing you're short of, Krystal," he reminded her.

She nodded with a grim smile. "That, and money."

"Yeah. Well, you be careful in dealing with Marcos. Make sure you're the one doing the convincing! The fact that he wants the land so badly automatically makes it worth more to you."

"But Jason, you know I don't care about that. I only want to be able to stay here."

"I know, hon. But selling may be your only choice. Anyway, it can't be the greatest place in the world for you to live. Aren't you lonesome way out there in the mountains?"

"No, Jason. I love it here. Taos is a wonderful place to be! You should see my view! It looks like a Christmas card here today! I don't want to even consider selling it."

"All right, Krystal. We'll discuss it later. You see what you can do from your side. But please keep me posted."

"I will, Jason. You'll be the first to know if anything important happens. You've always handled my business well. Even if you weren't my cousin, I would trust you implicitly."

He laughed at her open admiration. "That's nice to know, Krystal. Incidentally, you are coming down for Christmas with us, aren't you?"

"Oh, yes! I'll be there with bells on! Can't wait!"

"It should be an interesting experience for you. Christmas with twin four-year-olds! You'll be eager to fly back to your peaceful mountains after a few days!"

"I'm sure that's not so, Jason. I'm looking forward to being with you and Meg and the boys."

"Well, it'll liven up your holidays," he said with a laugh. "Things are never dull around our house, especially at Christmastime!"

"I'll see you next week, then."

"Okay." Jason sighed, sounding serious. "Krystal, please be careful when you're dealing with Marcos. The man is very powerful. He doesn't let anybody—or anything—get in his way. He is a ruthless man who goes after what he wants. And, hon, he wants your land!"

"Thanks for the warning, Jason," she murmured, fighting the urge to defend Gabe's character.

But deep inside Krystal worried that Jason was right. Already Gabe Marcos had proved his ability to get what he wanted—her! The only hitch to that theory was that she had wanted him, too. And it looked as though she was the one doing the pursuing. She had crashed the party. Knowing the risks, she had gone with him to his cabin. Then, disregarding the consequences, she had—oh, damn! With the toe of her boot she shoved two stacked boxes out of her way. The force sent them toppling into stacks of other boxes. She scrambled to straigthen them, mumbling to herself all the while.

The conversation with Jason had left Krystal unsettled, to say the least. She knew he was only trying to be practical when he talked about her selling the property. But he just didn't understand her need to be here. He couldn't possibly know why she had to be away.

Now here was a possible offer from Gabe Marcos. Of course Jason wanted to jump at it. He perceived the notion that she didn't give a whit about resale value as naive and unbusinesslike. Perhaps it was. But Krystal wanted to establish her business here in the Sangre de Cristo Mountains. Her new life.

Starting over was so hard to do. And this was the second time for Krystal. She was determined to make this one work. As if to prove her inner strength, she tore vigorously into one of the nearby boxes.

"Would you like a little help? Or some hot coffee?"

Krystal whirled at the sound of a man's gravelly voice. Then a smile replaced her startled expression. "Vegas! I could use help *and* a cup of coffee about now! Thank you. Please have a seat." She gratefully accepted the cup and motioned to a sturdy box.

The gray-haired man eased down and looked around at the mess of unpacked boxes. His gnarled hand swept to encompass the small building filled floor to ceiling with unopened boxes. "Is this going to be your gift shop?"

Krystal cringed at the words "gift shop." She cleared her throat and stated clearly, "This will be the boutique, Vegas. Ladies' clothes and specialty items. The art shop will be next door. I'd like to provide a place where local artisans can sell their wares. What do you think, Vegas? You could sell your metal sculpture here. Maybe you know of others who want to offer their art for sale."

The old man's dark eyes lifted to meet the young woman's green ones. He rubbed his chin thoughtfully. "Sure, I know some folks who'd be glad to bring things in here on consignment. But a coupla things got me puzzled."

"What's that?"

"Who you gonna sell them to?"

"Well." She chuckled at the honesty of his question. "I hope we'll be having customers soon. We aren't quite ready yet."

"No, you're not ready for much," he said, assessing the disorder around them. "I thought you were going to make this place a health-spa resort."

"Oh, I am," Krystal quickly affirmed. "It'll be a big complex when we're finished. These shops will just be a small part of the total structure. The other buildings need to be remodeled before they're ready. But since we already have this merchandise, we may as well open the shop first. As soon as we unpack the merchandise, we'll be ready for business. That is, if we can get the business to come to us. Right now they're by-passing our road for the one up the mountain to the ski resort."

"Yep," Vegas agreed. "This time of year, that's why they come up here. To go skiing down that damn-fool mountain." He shook his grizzled head as if he just couldn't understand such folly.

"Well," Krystal said as she smiled with satisfaction, "I'm going to see what I can do to change that. If we provide something else for them to do, like enjoy a health spa, maybe they'll come up here year-round."

Vegas shrugged heavy shoulders doubtfully. "Maybe . . ."

Krystal sipped the hot coffee, then turned to the older man. "Vegas, I know you're concerned about what the health spa will do to High Valley Ranch. I don't intend to destroy this beauty at all. I just want to be able to make a living up here in the mountains by utilizing what's here. It's as simple as that. It will be a place for all of us to live, just like it was when my uncle was here."

Vegas nodded and shifted on his seat. "When I agreed to stay on with you after Theo died, I knew there would be changes, Miss North. It jes' takes me awhile to get used to them. It was nice when he was here, and don't think I'm not grateful to him for all he did for me. But to be honest, nobody made much of a living here. Most people had to sell their stuff at rodeos and art shows all over the West. Some even traveled as far away as Houston."

Krystal was slightly surprised at his frank admission. "I'd like to be able to provide that opportunity to sell right here. Tourists always want local products. We wouldn't carry anything imported. Everything would be from New Mexican artisans."

"Sounds good," he said.

"Vegas, I do appreciate you staying on here with me at High Valley. It's nice to have someone close that I can trust and who knows all about this area. How long have you lived here?"

"Oh, about forty years. Came up from Las Vegas to learn blacksmithin'. Do you know where that is?" His eyes crinkled with a smile.

"Las Vegas? I'm assuming you're talking about the little town in New Mexico, not the gambling one in Nevada!" She laughed.

"Yep, that's the one." He nodded, delighted that she recognized the name of the little-known city. "I worked on most of the ranches around these parts over the years. Even spent some time working at the D. H. Lawrence Ranch before his widow, Frieda, gave it to the University of New Mexico."

Krystal smiled, wondering if Vegas had ever read any of Lawrence's work. "Oh, really, Vegas? Did you ever meet D.H. Lawrence?"

Vegas shrugged. "Naw. He was only here for a coupla years, anyway."

"When did you move here to High Valley?"

"I hurt my hip a few years back, and work was hard to come by. So I decided to put some of my scrap iron together and sell it to tourists in Taos. Theo came along and offered me room and board if I'd keep up repairs around this place. Plus I could continue sculpting in my spare time."

Krystal nodded. "That's exactly what I'd like you to do for me. Just keep the place running and flushing. Whatever you make in your metal shop can be sold right here, too. Would you help me locate other local artisans who want to sell their products?"

"Yes, ma'am."

"Vegas, please call me Krystal. We're going to be working too closely to remain formal." She smiled, and her emerald eyes glistened warmly. "Now let's unload some of this stuff and see what I have. It's left over from my shop in Albuquerque. I'm not even sure we can use any of it." Krystal set her cup aside and began rummaging in one box while Vegas dug into another.

They worked quietly for a while before Krystal gained the courage to ask, "Vegas, if you've lived here forty years, you must know Gabe Marcos at Starfire Ski Resort."

Vegas straightened and grew thoughtful for a moment. "Don't know Gabe. Knew his father, though. He was a rancher in these parts. A sheepherder. After he died, the family moved away."

"Gabe has had the ski resort for ten years, hasn't he?"

"Yep. I guess. I jes' never had the need to go up there on the mountain. He and Theo weren't exactly best friends, you know."

Krystal listened attentively. "So I understand. Why wouldn't my uncle sell to him?"

"Don't know about that. Jes' stubborn. Simply wanted to stay here. When young Gabe came back to Taos, he was intent on getting back all the land that used to be his family's ranch. It covered this whole valley and half the mountain where he put that ski resort."

Young Gabe? Krystal smiled to herself. He must be all of thirty-five or six. Aloud she pondered, "Maybe that's why he wants to buy this property so badly."

"Maybe"—Vegas chuckled roughly—"he jes' wants to add more property to his ski resort. That's sorta his own little world. He does whatever he wants to up there, and nobody can stop him."

Krystal raised her eyebrows. "What do you mean by that?"

"Oh, jes' rumors," he muttered. "They say if you really need a job, he'll get you one, no matter where you're from.

But you damn well better be ready to work hard. He don't cut no slack."

Krystal pressed her lips together thoughtfully. What was Vegas saying? Was there more to this than he was willing to say right now? Just what kind of person was Gabe Marcos? "I suppose we'd all better be prepared to work hard if we're going to make it," she assessed softly.

Vegas grinned. "You don't sound much like your uncle, Miss—er, Krystal."

She propped her hands on her hips. "I'm not much like my uncle, Vegas. Actually I didn't even know the man, but from the appearance of this place, he didn't bend his back working too hard!"

"No, he didn't!" Vegas chuckled. "He was content to struggle along, selling a painting or two here and there. Very easygoing fellow."

"I guess I'm just not that content, Vegas," Krystal said, peering outside at the sound of a vehicle pulling into the long driveway. "Well, speak of the devil," she muttered to herself.

A blue Bronco, by now familiar, halted before the small adobe building, and Gabe Marcos heaved his large body out. Long-legged strides had him in the doorway and knocking before Krystal could gather her wits. Then she was before him, opening the door to a gush of cold air and the man whose magic haunted her.

The December wind had tossed his black hair roughly and left his cheeks with a ruddy glow. His ski jacket hung open casually, as if the harsh New Mexico winter was no menace to him. His tight-legged, corded pants hugged taut thighs and tucked into heavy hiking boots. The incongruous part of him, those blue eyes, glistened brightly, and he smiled knowingly at her.

"What are you doing here so soon?" Krystal managed, then realized that she sounded perfectly asinine, not to mention downright unfriendly. Actually she was glad he had come. It meant their negotiations were still open, at least.

He shrugged angular shoulders. "I said I'd be in touch."

"So you did," Krystal admitted, gathering her calm. "Come on in. It's cold out there. I want you to meet my chief maintenance engineer, Vegas Santee. Vegas, this is Gabe Marcos." She prayed that Vegas wouldn't mention the embarrassing fact that they had just been discussing the tall man before them.

Vegas nodded and shook Gabe's hand without a word, eyeing the younger man solemnly.

"Vegas worked for my uncle and has agreed to stay on at High Valley and continue to work for me. He also makes beautiful metal sculptures," Krystal explained, trying to steer the conversation.

"Vegas . . . Vegas." Gabe pondered the name aloud. "I think I've seen your name somewhere. Maybe something around the lodge. Let me think . . . does a rough metal sunburst mounted on a wooden background sound familiar?"

Immediately Vegas's wrinkled face spread into a broad grin. "Yep! I made that sun about five years ago. But I remember it. How did you know?"

Gabe laughed and clapped him on the back. "Well, hell, man! I have your sculpture hanging in my office! You'll have to come up and see it sometime. I sit and stare at that thing when I'm having a problem. Then I end up wondering how the hell you made all those little twists and turns with hard metal to produce something so perfect. What skill! Not to mention patience!"

Krystal sighed with relief. The two men were instant friends. They exchanged a few more comments, then Gabe turned to Krystal. "I thought you could show me around."

No invitation, no questions—just a direct demand, delivered in such a way that Krystal was eager to accommodate. He had charmed her with one glance, but deep inside she knew it was because she wanted to be. He made her feel as no other man did and melted whatever resistance she tried to muster.

"Sure, Gabe. Vegas, you go ahead and do as much in here as you dare. I'll be back later to show you where it all goes. Just hang the dresses there and the belts over here." With an inward smile she grabbed her ski jacket. Krystal refused to let herself question why Gabe was there. She wanted to think it was a good sign, that he was considering her proposal, that he actually could be convinced, no matter what Jason said. She was happy to show him around. With pleasure! Maybe the convincing wouldn't be such an impossibility after all!

She stepped around the boxes and out into the crisp cold air with Gabe. There was something exhilarating about being with this man that sent Krystal's spirits soaring. Perhaps it was the hope he inspired within her. With his help, she would be able to achieve what she wanted in these mountains. Without it . . . she dreaded to think. It was doubtful that she would be able to recover financially —or emotionally. But she wouldn't think of that now.

"These three small buildings up front will be used for a group of shops and perhaps an office," Krystal explained as they walked together past the brown adobe structures. "The one we just left will be a boutique. In fact, we were just unloading some of my old stock from the shop in Albuquerque."

"Your shop?" It was surprising how much he didn't know about her, especially considering the intimacy they had shared.

"We—I ran a boutique in Albuquerque that specialized in women's clothes and accessories. Many were imports from South America, the kind that are so colorful and popular in the Southwest. But up here I'd like to specialize in New Mexican products, including some local art."

"Art?" he said harshly, his eyes as steely as his tone. "Did you know that Taos has more galleries per capita than anywhere else in the States?"

"No," she acknowledged slowly. "Does that mean there isn't room for one more?"

"Hell, Krystal, be reasonable. The market is swamped now! And here you are planning more touristy things!"

"No!" she protested. "Definitely not touristy things, as you call them! I want this entire resort to be a classy place, including the items for sale. They will be done in the tradition of Taos—well made, artistic and valuable. Vegas is going to help me. We're planning to provide a local artisans' market that will attract buyers from Texas, the larger New Mexican cities and other surrounding states." There was an indignance in her tone that caused Gabe to hush temporarily while he followed her past the next building.

"This one needs remodeling, as do some of the others," she commented, motioning. "There is no electricity. I don't know how Theo used some of these buildings. I think they just stood empty. But I intend to use them all."

"I'd like to see your idea for the health resort. I'm far

more interested in that than some fandangle boutiques," Gabe remarked somewhat caustically.

Krystal's emerald eyes snapped as she responded. "So am I! That's the main purpose of this entire complex. However, until a merger provides me the backing I need, I may be forced to live on the boutique and art shop. Believe me, that is not why I came to this ranch!"

Gabe caught her arm firmly. "Krystal, I just wanted to make sure you weren't planning a tourist-trap conglomeration here. I couldn't tolerate that!"

"Oh? And just what do you think you could do about it?" Krystal propped her fists on her hips angrily. The audacity of the man was infuriating! Just who did he think he was?

Those fierce blue eyes narrowed threateningly. "Believe me, Krystal, I'd find a way to stop you if I wanted to!"

There was something about the cold tone of his voice and his cutting glare that sent a shiver through her. Would he? In her mind at that moment there was no doubt. However, she defied him on principle. "You like to be in control, don't you, Mr. Marcos? Well, let me assure you that I will do whatever I want on *my land,* and you won't stop me! It just so happens that having a tourist trap is not what I'm planning for my business. But if it were, that is exactly what I would do! Now let go of my arm! You're hurting me!"

He eased his grip at her final words. "You are impossible!"

"Not as impossible as you, Gabe Marcos! I can't seem to get it through your head that my main concern here is building a health resort and spa that offer good nutrition, exercise and pampering!"

"Pampering?" He sneered incredulously.

Krystal folded her arms to calm her shaking hands. "Yes. Women like to be pampered. And this will be a place where they can be."

"For a price," Gabe added, his voice rough.

"Is skiing at Starfire free?" she countered.

"No," he admitted with a rueful smile.

"Well, neither is a health spa. But it will be reasonable. And that's more than I can say for you! Don't you understand, Gabe? I just want to be able to live here. Whatever I do with this place will be better than what it was before. I do not intend to make it any less than extraordinary—and very lovely. It will enhance this area—and your business as well—if we work together. It will bring tourists, yes; but so does your resort. What's wrong with that?" She could feel the emotion rising within her and feared the unthinkable—tears! She fought them from deep within. The last thing she wanted to do in front of him was cry. She had to show him her strength.

Gabe sighed heavily, exasperatingly, after her outburst and looked away from her convincing, intense eyes. Perhaps he just didn't want to hear her reasons for wanting to stay here. They were the wrong reasons, anyway. None was as strong or as meaningful as his. He gazed over the far reaches of High Valley Ranch, seeing endless stretches of land that looked and smelled differently from any place on earth. None had such a hold on him as this oak- and aspen-covered place.

"I suppose you're right, Krystal." His voice was strangely quiet. "It's just that I had to be sure about a new person coming into this valley and what you intended to do with it. This land means more to me than just adjoining acreage. It—it was once part of my family's sheep ranch."

"Oh?" Krystal looked up at him, grateful that he was

at last being truthful with her. But that in no way committed her to complete honesty with him. "Is that why you're so attached to this place?"

He looked at her sharply. "I am not so attached—hey, are you going to show me these other buildings or do we have to stand out here and freeze?"

"Sure." Krystal turned on her heel and led the way into the largest of the empty adobe buildings. If he wanted to continue playing games, she would! "This will be the main exercise room."

Their footsteps echoed on bare concrete floors. Brown log beams gave the place an authentic old-territory look, and windows on either side opened to the wooded areas surrounding the lodge. As rough as it now looked, there was definite potential in the room. In fact, everything she had said so far made sense.

Gabe's voice mellowed, and he turned an amused face toward her. "So this is where you switch on the bouncy music and everyone dances and hops around to the beat, losing those unwanted pounds?"

Krystal looked at him quizzically for a moment. "What? Oh, I know what you mean! Aerobics!"

"Yes, that's what it's called."

"Actually it's very good for you, and we'll probably include an aerobics class in one of the smaller rooms. This room will be full of exercise equipment. We'll design specific programs for each client. Of course, there'll be other strenuous activities, but that's where you come in, Gabe."

"Me? Forget it! I don't know anything about all those machines!"

"Oh, I didn't mean that you'd be running the machines or leading exercises." She laughed.

"Good! You had me worried for a minute!" He cast her

a teasing glance. "Actually I have my own techniques for keeping fit."

"I'll bet you do," she retorted sarcastically. "Those guests that want to and are physically fit can catch a bus here that will take them directly up to your resort for a day of skiing. I won't be providing what you already offer. And vice versa, I hope. Here, let me show you."

Taking his arm, Krystal steered Gabe to the small front office, where a map lay sprawled across the desk. His eyes became riveted on the flat surface that reduced the magnificent mountain and highland valley to a flat, discernible surface where one could see every hidden arroyo and stream. He watched her finger trace an almost-straight line from the area where they now stood to Starfire Ski Resort. On paper it was a simple matter. One could see where the dangerous hairpin-curved road could be eliminated completely. It did make sense, especially from her point of view. However, would he be giving up too much?

Gabe pressed his lips together. Perhaps he should end her hopes now, before either of them went any further. His eyes raked over the entire map from the bottom, at High Valley Ranch, to the top, where Starfire covered the entire mountaintop. "Krystal—"

"Isn't it exciting? I knew you would be impressed if you took the time to study it, Gabe. See how wonderful it could be? The road is a simple matter, and it only makes sense." Her emerald eyes sparkled with enthusiasm.

"Yes, well . . ." Gabe raked his hand over his chin.

"Come on, Gabe. The best is out here." Krystal smiled in gentle persuasion. "I'll show you the hot springs."

A distant look veiled his eyes briefly, but he followed her without a word.

"All this will be decked and covered, so the spa area will

connect with the main exercise rooms," Krystal explained as she hopped from the back porch to the snow-covered yard. Leading the way, Krystal was too preoccupied with her own thoughts to notice Gabe's reaction as they covered each additional foot of land.

His sharp eyes measured the rocky hillside, the stand of bare silvery aspens, the spread of water oaks. Inhaling the familiar fragrance of moist pines, Gabe was overwhelmed with memories . . .

Krystal scrambled eagerly through huge boulders, around fat-trunked oak trees, disappearing in the direction of the sound of gurgling water. By the time he joined her, she was hunched on a flat rock, gazing expectantly into the misty water of a small pool. Faint wisps of grayish vapor rose to meet the crisp winter air. "Isn't it beautiful here?" She smiled up at him with the innocence of a child who had just discovered a treasure. And indeed she had. *His treasure!*

"Yes—yes, it's very nice," he commented vaguely, entranced with the moment and the memories.

"Come on over here, Gabe. Feel the water. It's naturally warm!" she encouraged.

Gabe approached the water slowly, almost reverently, and stooped beside her to touch its ripples with apprehensive fingers.

Krystal searched his face, watching the angular structure set in firm, harsh lines. What was he thinking? There was a quietness between them, a oneness with the place, with the moment. They belonged here, both of them, together. "Have you ever been here before, Gabe?"

His voice was strained. "Yes, of course. But it's been a long time."

Krystal dipped her hand into the water and sent a ripple

across the surface. "They say the Indians came here for healing ceremonies. Do you suppose the warm water has special powers?" She would never have believed it before this moment. But now, with Gabe Marcos, anything was possible.

He shrugged. After a long silence, he answered, "This is a special place, Krystal. A little magic . . ."

"When we build the spa, I want to keep this area as close to what it is now as we can," Krystal speculated dreamily. "I want the building constructed around these rocks and trees. Of course, we'll have to pipe the water into the pool."

Gabe looked around, trying to imagine a building surrounding the wild, natural spot. He shuddered inside at the prospect of people invading this place. Would it be possible to do what she said—to keep it natural and refrain from destroying its beauty with new construction? Bulldozers, engineers, construction crews, swarms of tourists—it all spelled destruction to him.

". . . not without your help. Gabe? Are you listening?"

"What? Oh, yes! What did you say, Krystal?"

"Gabe! I said that I couldn't do all this without your help. I need to know who can design the right kind of building and who can build it. I also want your opinions as it's being constructed."

"And my money!" Gabe countered.

"No! All I need is your backing, your countersignature on the note. I have good credit and can get the loan myself, but not without substantially more collateral. The loan will be my indebtedness. I swear it, Gabe. We can add a clause to that effect in the contract," she urged sincerely.

"Contract? Krystal, you're moving too fast. I'm still mulling over the idea. It's too new and bizarre."

"It's not bizarre! It's normal business! People in business do it every day! It just makes sense—good business sense! We'll cooperate to make it work well for both of us. You get your road through my property; I get my loan. And we share the year-round profits!"

"I have to think on it, Krystal. The problem's not that easily resolved. This land is—was—mine. I want it back." His blue eyes were glazed with steel.

Krystal couldn't help countering his one-sided reasoning. "It's not for sale. First, it wasn't yours; it was your father's. And who among us has everything that once belonged to our families? Now the place is mine, Gabe Marcos, for whatever reasons. It's all I have in the world, and I intend to keep it. You can either work with me and become a partner or kiss this land good-bye!" Oh, God, she wished her bluff were solid truth!

Gabe moved closer to where Krystal sat on the rock. She could feel his masculine virility, his power. Who did she think she was, speaking to this man so boldly? Did she want to ruin everything? Alienate him completely? She would never be able to manage in the mountains without his support.

His lips were very close, faintly smiling. "I'll take that kiss—but not the good-bye."

Without further warning Gabe made good his claim with a kiss so savage, so untamed, that Krystal was swept breathlessly into a spontaneous response. Out of mind was their immediate conversation. Forgotten was their business encounter. There was only awareness of lips melding with lips and a crushing embrace. They clung mercilessly, transformed by the sizzling union and sheer physical magnetism to another time.

The wild, undomesticated setting provided the background for the clandestine coming together of the two lovers, one dark and rugged, the other blond and irresistible. He was unrelenting in his passion. She was his captive. Yet their coming together was a sweet mixture of giving and taking. She opened her lips to his, inviting him seductively to taste her sweetness. She met his tongue with her own in daring temptation. She raised her chin wantonly as his lips rippled down the creamy column of her neck, pausing for his darting tongue to trace sensuous patterns on her skin. She wanted to feel his kisses all over her, know the gentle nip of his white teeth on soft places, savor his masculinity.

From the depths of her mind Krystal knew a feeble moment of protest. Gabe's lips moved back to hers, smothering the weak plea. He ignited in her a smoldering passion that had never been completely doused since the first night they met—and made love. Krystal was trapped by the power, the wonderful magic of Gabe Marcos! A low, animallike moan escaped her lips, and she awakened to the struggle of her own body against his.

"Gabe, please . . ." she breathed.

"Ah, Krystal, don't you see what you do to me? We both feel it," he growled against her skin, pulling her tighter against him.

"I . . . don't think . . . this should go any further, Gabe," Krystal begged, trying to regain control of the situation and her own wild emotions. "You know this can't continue. We have business—"

"Never mix business with pleasure." His voice rasped against her ear as his lips nibbled at the sensitive lobe. "You have nice ears, *mi joyalita* . . . kiss me."

A shiver of raw desire raked uncontrolled through her body at his pleasurable touches. She wanted to enjoy the moment. Oh, how she wanted him! But she didn't dare! Not again! "No!" Was that her shrill voice?

"Don't stop now, Krystal."

She pushed roughly against his chest. "Gabe, let me up! I don't want this to happen again."

Her words struck him sharply, and he relinquished his hold. "Krystal, don't say that. The magic is still here with us. Surely you feel it."

She reached to smooth her hair. "We—we can't yield to it again, Gabe. We just can't. There are other things to consider now. When you're ready to talk about the merger, I'll see you again." She rose and stumbled numbly over the rocks that hid the natural springs from the rest of the world. She had to get away from him and break this spell or she would never be able to resist—and would never accomplish what she had to.

"Krystal!" His tone halted her. "Krystal, let's talk. Tomorrow night. Over dinner."

Slowly she turned to look at him. Would she never be able to resist him? Already she had responded to his kiss, much to her chagrin. She was aware that she spoke to him one way yet reacted in quite another. Inside, her feminine emotions were raging. Could he tell?

"I'd like to take you to Taos for dinner. It's especially beautiful this time of year. We can—talk then."

She took a breath. "Okay," she agreed, not really sure why. It was a bribe, and she knew it.

He caught up with her and reached for her hand. Together they walked back over the rocky earth. Little was said between them, but the gesture was tender, perplexing Krystal even further. She watched with wistful eyes as he drove away in the blue Bronco. Was she making a mistake? Should she attempt to keep this relationship with Gabe strictly business? Or was it too late for that?

Suddenly words of warning from Jason flashed before her. "He is a ruthless man who goes after what he wants. And, hon, he wants your land!" Grimly she pressed her lips together. Well, maybe, Mr. Gabriel Marcos, you have met your match!

CHAPTER FOUR

Krystal peered out the window for the seventeenth time, then straightened and fidgeted nervously with her blouse. He was late, damnit, and she was pacing the floor like a smitten teenager!

It had taken her half an hour to decide what to wear. Should she dress pragmatically in a suit, stylishly black with a cranberry blouse? This was a business dinner, wasn't it? Or should she wear the low-cut green dress that matched her eyes? A bit too dramatic, probably. Perhaps she should go with the sporty ski-scene look in Nordic sweater and stretchy pants. In the end she had taken a middle-of-the-road approach, choosing gray wool slacks that hugged her hips and a tailored red silk blouse. Red was one of her best colors, and she felt good wearing it. A waist-length fur jacket and pant-boots completed her attire. Her blond hair curled casually at her shoulders, giving a feminine flair to her appearance.

Again she searched the black night for headlights. Where was he? A little tingle spun through her at the thought of being with Gabe Marcos once more. He was an overwhelming personality. She seemed to lose control with him, something that disturbed her. Deep down she feared being swayed by him. And yet she couldn't wait to see him, to be with him again.

She bent to the window again. There they were—the lights that signaled his arrival! Taking a deep breath,

her response was from the heart. "No, Gabe, it
bad at all." Krystal's breath caught in her throat
admission. *Bad?* Oh dear God, it was wonderful!
rm stretched across the back of her seat, and long
slid under her hair to caress her nape softly. "Krys-
on't know why, but I—that is—our night together
ial in my memory. Can you believe that?" He
d the steering wheel tightly. What was he trying to
e'd had women before and never felt the need to
his feelings. How could he tell her clearly how he
ien he didn't know himself?
stal's heart pounded, and she glanced through the
ess at him. Her eyes fell on his large hands, white-
led and tense. She loved the sensitive touch of those
le hands yet feared her own wild responses to them.
es, I think so," she answered softly, hoping he spoke
ely and that she wasn't reading too much into his
ient. She watched snow-laden trees whiz by silently,
ere seemed nothing more to say as the two of them
ed the magic of that night.
uh, hope you're hungry tonight," Gabe offered final-
We're having the best steak in Taos."
ctually I am." She smiled, relieved to be discussing
thing—*anything*—else. "Where are we going?"
oc Martin's Restaurant. It's located in the Taos Inn.
you heard of it?"
o."
was a private residence for years. Just recently it was
vated and placed on the register of National Historic
. The style is typical of old Taos construction. It may
you some ideas on how you'd like the buildings at
Valley to look."
rystal raised her eyebrows. Was he suggesting that she

Krystal steeled herself against the biting cold of the New Mexican night and the man whose company she would keep. Gabe was excitingly handsome tonight in sweater, jacket and slacks all in shades of brown. He stood in her doorway, outlined against the white background like a warrior whose memories and dreams are hidden behind a spartan mask. Then he smiled, and Krystal walked over to him with a grin.

Gabe held the door politely while she slid into the warm interior of the Bronco. He eased into the driver's seat beside her. Before starting the motor, he looked at her, admiration clearly written on his face.

"You know something? This is our first real date!" He chuckled, obviously delighted with the thought, but Krystal squirmed inside. She was embarrassingly aware of the intimacy they had shared before their "first date."

"It's time we got to know each other, don't you think?" she offered with a shy smile.

His tanned hand touched her pink cheek lightly. "High time. You're very pretty tonight, Krystal. Sorry I'm late. The road was hell tonight—ice patches everywhere. It took me longer than I expected to travel down the resort road, then back up here to High Valley."

Krystal seized the moment he had so handily provided. "I understand completely. It's too bad we don't have a road that connects our property. It would certainly be more convenient—and a lot safer."

He gave her a sardonic glance. "Almost the first words out of the lady's mouth! Are you going for the jugular tonight? I had hoped we could have a pleasant evening together and get to know each other, since we're such *friendly* neighbors. Can't you forget your damn business for a little while?"

"Are you forgetting business, Gabe?" Somehow she doubted if he ever did.

"With a lovely woman like you by my side? Of course!" He smiled.

"Please, Gabe. Let's drop the pretenses. You and I both know why we're here."

His face was a sculpture of angular shadows in the semidarkness, but Krystal could see the firm setting of his jaw as he retorted, "Why *are* we here, Krystal? Somehow I thought I was going out with an attractive woman who interested and challenged me. I'm here because I want to get to know you better."

"The challenge being to see if you can change my mind about starting a business here on *your* mountain!"

"If that's what you think, why did you come tonight?"

She smiled wryly and answered honestly. "I'm not sure. Perhaps I wondered if we could ever get along enough to consider a business merger. Just curious, you understand."

"I'm curious, too, Krystal. Curious about this woman who has entered my life so boldly and is attempting to entangle me in her life." His long fingers lifted a golden strand of hair from her shoulder and wrapped it sensuously into a coil.

She could feel the heat of his skin close to her cheek and the gentle tug on her hair. "Gabe," she began. "Please understand that I only want a business relationship with you. Once we were caught up in something beyond our control. Now I'm afraid you see me as someone very different from who I really am."

He pulled gently on the curl, and her head inclined toward him. "For your information, I don't usually suc-

cumb to a woman's charms so q
pursuit."

"Am I supposed to be impres
ingly close to her.

His finger caressed her cheek. "
wrong impression of me. Maybe
other straight."

"I thought we were going to di

"Let's forget business tonight a
It's nearly Christmas, and the lig
beautiful. It will be special—and s

Krystal eyed him satirically, wei
was certainly blunt. But then so wa
hit upon raw nerves, and they had
minutes. Now he was calling a truce
being gullible, but the idea appealed
agreed. No business tonight." She wa
by his very presence.

"Good." His hand slid beneath the
and pulled her even closer. Their li
velvety caress. Then he moved and shi
gear. As they began to roll forward, he
"Krystal . . ." There was a moment
listened to the crunch of heavily stu
snowy road.

She struggled for a calmness she c
after his easy kiss. "Yes?"

His voice was heavy and strange in
wasn't so bad that night. Or was it m

What was he saying? He wanted appr
on their night of passion! She wanted to
who had awakened her that night to lon
and perhaps compromised her future.

instead
wasn't
at the
His
fingers
tal, I
is spe
gripp
say?
explai
felt w
Kr
dark
knuc
capa
"Y
since
com
for t
reca
"I
ly. "
"
som
"
Hav
"
"
ren
Site
give
Hig
K

actually would be renovating High Valley? At times she doubted the possibility. "It seems like I'll be redoing more than I originally planned. The ceiling fell in today, and we had to repack all those boxes in the boutique."

"What?"

Krystal shook her head woefully. "The minute we get one thing fixed, another falls apart. Snow caved in the roof and ruined some of my stock. Vegas and I spent the day cleaning up the mess. Now I need to get someone to help repair it. Do you know anyone I could hire?"

"Of course, Krystal. You should have called me. We have a maintenance crew who can take care of anything. I'll be glad to help you. In fact, I'll send them down first thing tomorrow."

"Thanks, Gabe. Vegas is an excellent repairman, but construction just isn't his field."

"Still, you're lucky to have him."

"Yes, I am. He was the only one from my uncle's art colony who wanted to stay on and work for me. Even though they all had that option, no one else could live with my one stipulation—that they contribute something besides art. I need workers right now. Art will have to be in the future."

Gabe grinned in the darkness. "You drive a hard bargain, don't you?"

"You bet. No one gets a free ride. But isn't that the way you work, Gabe?" She knew he did from what Vegas had told her.

"Oh, I agree with you completely, Krystal. Everybody must work in order to reap the rewards. I like your ideas. You have a good—head on your shoulders."

"You almost said 'good business head,' didn't you?" she teased.

"Yeah," he admitted ruefully. "Good business head."

She sighed with satisfaction at his admission. "Here we go, talking about business. And after our deal."

"Sorry," he said. "I guess that was my fault. It seems to creep in. I just hope you realize the unpredictability of the tourist trade. It's tough, especially up here in these mountains."

"I know about the tourist trade, Gabe. Thanks for your concern," Krystal answered in a clipped tone. He was determined to get in his jabs, she fumed to herself.

They rode along in dark silence until the Christmas lights of Taos were visible. Before them, *farolitas* lined streets and edged square adobe roofs. The small paper bag lanterns glowed brightly from stepped brick walls, creating a unique Southwestern Christmas splendor. They drove slowly down Placitas Road and around Taos Plaza, where everything was outlined with the golden lights.

Gabe breathed with satisfaction. "The whole place takes on a special look, doesn't it?"

Krystal smiled warmly. "Oh, yes. I love it. The *luminarias* are so beautiful."

"We purists in the northern part of the state call them *farolitas. Luminarias* are those small log bonfires that are lit on Christmas Eve," he explained as they pulled to a stop in front of the Taos Inn.

"Purists in the north! Ha!" Krystal laughed teasingly. "Nothing here is pure. The traditions, even the people are a blending of Spanish, Indian, Mexican and Anglo."

He switched off the motor and turned his attention to her, his presence looming large and overpowering and darkly handsome. "I like it that way. The blending makes things interesting."

She smiled nervously. "It's part of what makes Taos so special."

"The blending makes things interesting for people, too," he whispered huskily. "Like you and me . . ." His hand stroked her cheek gently and cupped her chin. "We're so different, but we blend nicely." A kiss was so close she could almost feel it.

"Gabe . . ." She swallowed noticeably. "Don't you think we'd better go in?" She was falling, drowning again, but she fought it determinedly this time.

His eyes assessed her, though again he hid his thoughts. "Sure."

She struggled to deny the attraction between them. It was her only defense. Otherwise she would succumb to Gabe's power over her. In one sweeping movement he was out of the vehicle, and she was with him. Through the cold, dark air, the beautifully appropriate strains of "Winter Wonderland" from a lone classical guitar reached them.

Krystal was still slightly shaken as Gabe steered her into the classic Southwestern interior. They went first into the Adobe Bar, where Gabe requested that they be seated in the balcony overlooking the two-story lobby. It provided complete privacy.

She sat across from him, studying the play of flickering lights across his swarthy cheeks from the *farolitas.* Gabe Marcos was certainly impressive, bordering on handsome tonight in his russet turtleneck sweater and tan herringbone jacket. His skin, a sweet ginger color, glistened invitingly, and she flushed as she remembered the unforgettable sizzle of his brown-skinned body against hers. His hair was dark, close to jet, and so were his brows. They gave him an authoritarian air. His features were durable and masculine, just like the man—a straight nose, sensitive lips, an angular chin that jutted a bit too much, made him irresistible. The only incongruous part in his determined face was those deep blue eyes. Oh yes, she could easily drown in their depths again.

The waiter stood politely at their table, and Gabe leaned forward, interrupting her musings. "Krystal, what will you have?"

"A wine spritzer, please," she answered.

He gave his order of Seven and 7 to the waiter and, folding his arms on the table, leaned toward her. "Okay, tell me about the real Krystal North."

"What do you want to know?" His bluntness had caught her off guard.

"Whatever you want me to know. Tell me about your marriage."

Gabe had given her an option while steering her in a certain direction. He was distinctly in control. Yet this was an area she wouldn't mind telling him about. Her marriage could be summed up rather succinctly. "It was a mistake. We both realized it within a year, although we held on and tried to make it work for three. When he got a job offer in California, I decided not to go. The divorce was a mutual agreement, with little disturbance."

"No children?"

She shook her head, and her golden hair shimmered. "Thank goodness we realized that children would not solve our marital problems." She bent her head to sip the wine before her. "And you?"

"What? Kids? Who, me?" He seemed startled at the thought.

She smiled at his reaction. "Have you ever been married?"

He pressed his lips tightly together. "No. I—it just never happened. I've been too busy, I guess."

Too busy? From some of the tales she'd heard, Krystal knew what he'd been busy doing! Why would he want to be confined to marriage when he was king of the mountain and could have any woman he wanted? Including her! "So I've heard," she admitted aloud, then castigated herself. She couldn't believe she had said that to him.

"Oh, and what have you heard?" he urged.

Krystal decided she had started something that she had better finish. She tried to do it in a teasing manner. Arching one eyebrow, she confessed, "I've heard that you have a very, ah, vivid personal life and are never wanting for female companionship."

"Vivid personal life? What the hell is that supposed to mean?"

"That you can have any woman you want—" She said it begrudgingly.

He shifted closer, his knee resting intimately against hers. "Right now you are the only woman I want, Krystal. And I can't seem to get my hands on you!"

He appeared to be dead serious, and she didn't want to fall into that trap of denial again. With a wry smile she added, "From my experience, Mr. Marcos, I'm inclined to agree with those rumors."

He countered with a jab of his own. "Look, mysterious lady, from *my* experience, you are the seductive witch of the north. Pity the poor weak male who stands in your way! I happened to be one of the victims!" He was teasing her, and the gleam in his eyes was priceless. She couldn't help responding.

"Victims? Why, you—you're the one who invited me to your cabin, for heaven's sake!" Her emerald eyes flashed at him across the table. Strains of "O Holy Night" sounded beautifully in the background.

"Who seduced whom? Look who crashed my party that night! And no one forced you into anything! You were quite willing!" The devil danced in his blue eyes.

Krystal clamped her jaw shut. He was right! Perhaps she had led him on. And she certainly hadn't resisted very strongly. In the end she had wanted him every bit as much as he had wanted her. How could she deny it? Her eyes lifted to meet his. A small smile played at the corners of her lips.

"Witch of the north, huh?" She grinned broadly, and soon they were laughing together. It was the break, the mellowing of mood they both needed if they were to survive the evening. "You'd better watch out for Wicked Witch North! She's out to get innocent men!" Krystal raised both hands in a threatening gesture, teasing and taunting.

Gabe, delighted with her playfulness, grabbed both wrists, pulling them to his waist. His lips were dangerously close to hers as he murmured, "My beautiful witch, I'm enchanted by your charms. Innocent and naive though I am . . ." He nuzzled her ear with sensuous whispers.

"You? Innocent and naive?" she scoffed laughingly.

"I'm completely vulnerable. Teach me, Krystal." His lips nibbled lightly along her jawline.

"Not a chance!"

"Then let me teach you," he offered wickedly.

"Gabe—" she protested and tried to wriggle out of his grasp. "Someone will see us." She could feel the warmth of his chest and longed to run her hands over the smooth muscles there.

With slow reluctance he released his grip, allowing her

to scoot away. His eyes captured her with conviction of his promise. "All right, Witchy, just wait till later."

She smoothed her hair with a shaky hand. "Your threats don't scare me. A witch isn't easily intimidated."

"Do witches get hungry? Ready to go into the dining room for dinner?" Gabe offered.

"I'm starved!" she exclaimed.

"Why didn't you tell me?"

"Why didn't you ask?"

"Since when did you ever wait to be asked, Krystal? You're a woman who goes after what she wants." He rose and helped her with her chair.

She cast a sideways glance at Gabe. Those were the very words Jason had used to describe him. It was strange to hear them applied to her. After all, she and Gabe were so different. Or were they?

Krystal glided down the stairs from their private balcony at Gabe's side, her spirits buoyed by their laughter. It had been so long since she had laughed . . . and loved. Oh, what was she thinking? She couldn't let this happen! But she couldn't deny the wonderful feelings she had when she was with him. Was that so bad? No, she decided and clung to his arm as they sailed through the high-ceilinged lobby with its twenty-foot stripped-log *vigas,* past the beautiful fountain, formerly the old town well. When they were seated, Gabe chose to be next to her, not across the table.

Krystal smiled happily at him. This was where she wanted him to be—close. His warmth, his energy, his masculine fragrance permeated the air, and she just wanted to absorb it all. Oh, God, she was swirling again, right into Gabe Marcos's arms. But she didn't care.

"A little wine with dinner?" he suggested.

She nodded, her emerald eyes aglow.

Gabe ordered for them, then gestured at their surroundings. "Don't you like the traditional pueblo style of the place?"

"I love the beehive fireplaces and the *vigas.* You're right, Gabe. High Valley could easily be renovated like this. And it would be so appropriate!" She was encouraged that he had again broached the subject.

"Would you stick to the traditional woman's role in such an endeavor?"

"Woman's role?" Krystal bristled instantly at the notion, conjuring the image of a woman—herself—in the kitchen.

He smiled, and she melted a little. "It's not what you think. In the old days the woman did the finishing plaster on an adobe house and its *horno,* the beehive-shape oven or fireplace. She was called an *enjarradora,* and the tradition still exists today."

"Sounds interesting." Krystal smiled at the suggestion. "I'd have to learn to do it, but I'd like that."

"I'm sure someone right here in Taos could teach you. In fact, the *enjarradora* who capped these walls built an *horno* at the Smithsonian Institution in Washington. So we have an expert right here in our midst."

"How exciting! Yes, I'd like to meet her and see what we can work out." Krystal looked more closely at the walls around her. "I can imagine it would be quite a satisfying job."

Gabe's finger caressed her hand. "It's very hard work, Krystal. Why, you might even rough up those pretty hands."

"These pretty hands are accustomed to hard work, Gabe Marcos. What do you think I did today when the roof caved in?"

"I wish you had called me."

She shrugged. "Why should I? I'm not used to having a man around to help me. I'm grateful that Vegas is there."

"Do you mean that men weren't swarming around to help you in Albuquerque?" He raised an eyebrow.

"No, my sister and I handled most things ourselves. After my divorce, I was determined to make it on my own. I thought I didn't need a man's help."

"And you were unapproachable," he concluded. "I find that hard to believe, Krystal. Anyone as pretty as you should have men at your beck and call."

She shook her head. "I had a few—friends. But I guess I just threw myself into the work at the shop. I didn't want to get seriously involved with another man. My work was most important at the time."

"And now?" he asked, nonchalantly drinking his wine.

She tried to meet his evasive eyes. What was he getting at? "I have even more work now than ever," she said quietly. "And I've already thrown myself into it."

"You were in partnership with your sister in Albuquerque, weren't you?"

She angled her head at him. "Yes, but how did you know that?"

"I did some checking on you," he admitted, touching her wrist to soften the harshness of the statement.

She bristled anyway. "Checking up on me? Why?"

His fingers stroked her skin softly. "I want to know more about my neighbor. You don't expect me to consider a business deal with a complete stranger—almost complete, that is."

She held her breath, apprehensive but hopeful. "Are you considering?"

The gentle stroking stopped. "Standard business procedures. Just preliminary, of course."

"Of course." She smiled confidently. It was a good sign. "What else did you find out?"

"That you have a superior record. You paid your bills regularly. You had an excellent small business until your sister died. After that, profits dwindled. You finally dissolved the defunct partnership. Shortly after the inheritance of High Valley Ranch, you sold the shop." He stopped and took a deep breath.

There was some relief in Krystal's eyes. "That just about sums it up." She nodded, praying he hadn't pried further. She would gladly show him her profit-and-loss statements, her bookkeeping records, anything about the business he wanted to see.

"I'm inclined to think that's just surface information about you, Krystal." His eyes reflected a seriousness she hadn't seen before.

She laughed lightly, trying to be convincing. "Not really. I led a pretty dull life."

"Tell me about your sister," he encouraged gently.

She sighed and looked down at her hands, fidgeting with the goblet on the table, trying to ignore his touch on her wrist. "There isn't much to tell. She died of a rare bone cancer last year."

"How old was she?"

"Twenty-six."

"God, that's young! I know it must have been hard for you. I'm—sorry, Krystal." His hand covered hers warmly, securely. His tone was genuinely sympathetic.

"Yes," she admitted in a loud whisper. "It was an extremely difficult year. In fact, that's probably why I jumped at the chance to come to High Valley. I felt that

I just had to get away from the shop, and Albuquerque, and everything that reminded me of Margo. Opening the shop day after day was almost unbearable. Many times I just didn't. Of course, profits dropped. And for a while I didn't even care."

"I think I can understand," Gabe said. "So the inheritance came at a perfect time for you."

"It was a godsend," she stated quietly but firmly.

"I'm sure it was." He moved his hand from hers as their plates were set before them.

They turned their attention to the meal, and although small talk was exchanged, the seriousness of their previous conversation had set a different tone to the evening.

"The steak is great, Gabe. And prepared just the way I like it—medium-rare." Krystal smiled contentedly. "Even the music is perfect tonight."

They could now see the guitarist who had serenaded them all evening. He was young but a very accomplished musician. His long, slender fingers skimmed rapidly over the strings to produce melodies that alternated between traditional Christmas music and fiery Spanish-sounding tunes.

"I don't recognize some of those words, Gabe. What is he saying?" whispered Krystal when the young man began to sing in accompaniment to his guitar. The fluid Spanish language flowed like velvet enchantment from his lips.

Gabe leaned close, his shoulder pressing hers, his lips near her ear. "*A ojos verdes traicioneros* . . . treacherous green eyes . . . *suspirando por tu amor* . . . I spend every night sighing for your love."

She looked doubtfully at Gabe, then smiled warmly. It was wonderful to be with him, to imagine that he was singing the song to her, that he wanted her love. "The singer has a very romantic voice."

Gabe smiled. "I thought you would like him. Actually, I prefer his sister's act. She'll be out shortly."

Soon the guitarist strummed a fanfare, and a beautiful young woman entered the small stage area. With her head and arms held high, she stood poised in the center before starting her dance.

"Flamenco!" Krystal breathed excitedly. "Ohhhh . . ."

Every eye focused on the woman's perfect hourglass form and the haughty lift to her chin. Her dark hair was pulled back tightly in a chignon, and a single rose adorned one ear. It was all part of the act, but the audience loved it. The girl's feet moved rapidly, pounding an exciting, compelling beat while her hands and arms lifted expressively. Arching her lithe body seductively, she flipped the brilliant ruffles of her skirt below the knees and twirled in grand Spanish style.

At the end the diners applauded loudly, realizing what a rare treat they had been exposed to. Shouts of "Bravo!" and "Bellissimo!" filled the restaurant.

Gabe beamed like a proud father. "This is a limited engagement. The Santa Fe Opera is interested, and they will be auditioning there in a few weeks."

"Oh, we're so lucky to have seen and heard them!" Krystal said. "But how do you know so much about them? Are they friends of yours?"

"You might say I'm their only friend in the States. They're a brother-and-sister act I met in Málaga last year when I was in Spain. Their father and I made an—arrangement, and I agreed to bring them here and try to boost their careers. I feel very strongly that they're talented and deserve all the best or I wouldn't have bothered."

"How generous of you," Krystal murmured, wondering about this man who claimed not to have time for developing a relationship with a wife but managed to go to Spain and boost the careers of performing artists.

"It's not pure generosity, I can assure you," Gabe admitted. "It's business, *mi querida,* good business."

She stiffened, for it occurred to her that so was this evening. "Is everything business to you, Gabe?"

He kissed the small lobe of her ear. "No, Krystal. Not everything. Not tonight. Tonight is special."

Later Krystal paced the dark room alone, remembering. Would she ever be able to forget him? Could she possibly? Not as long as her mind was awake! Awake and filled with thoughts of the evening with Gabe. She was infatuated, while he was dealing business. Why couldn't she control her feelings? But already she had ruined it all. *What now?*

She recalled the velvety caress of his lips and found herself whirling again into the bottomless eddy that overwhelmed her whenever she was near Gabe, whenever he touched her. She imagined herself clinging to him, allowing his kiss to deepen. She was willing—again—to fall into his arms. She could almost feel him hovering near her in the darkness.

Her mind was playing tricks on her. It was as if he were really there!

Her emotions were real enough, though. She could feel him lying with her, his body branding hers with fire, teasing her with his masculinity. He covered her with his dark form, outlined against the night, and she received him eagerly. Or did she? Oh God, her imagination was going wild! She recalled with clarity every word, every sizzling touch . . .

"Krystal, it can be special again. I want to make love to you, *mi joyalita.*" His lips blazed liquid fire down the ivory column of her neck and beyond. Her breasts grew taut with anticipation of his touch.

Her own voice was a hollow sound. "No, Gabe, please! We'll ruin everything. This is not for us!"

"I want you, *mi querida.* Now! Don't deny this special magic, Krystal." His lips roamed over her with fierce promises of desire's fulfillment.

She pushed at his chest, knowing that if he wanted to, he could easily overpower her. "No!" she said, her words muffled against his lips. "We can't. We have other things to consider. You promised! The business—"

"To hell with business!" His voice rumbled against her. "There is nothing to consider tonight but us, Krystal."

The air was cold against her flushed face, and suddenly Krystal wasn't sure what was real and what she was imagining. She only knew one thing: She had sent him away—and she was now alone.

As she lay awake and alone during the long, cold night, she recalled her denial with deep, gnawing regret. How she could have done it was beyond her. And why? Because now she wanted him to hold her close, to feel his warmth, to know his love throughout the night. But it was too late.

CHAPTER FIVE

Krystal squinted in the bright New Mexico sun as she made her way up the treacherous mountain road. New snow blanketed the ground, and more was predicted. It would ensure a beautiful Christmas and encourage skiing. But what would it matter to her? It was Gabe's business that would improve, not hers. She *had* no business . . . and might never have one!

Gabe's secretary, a pretty woman with dark, oval eyes and a thick braid down her back, steered Krystal into his office. "I'll try to locate him, Miss North. I'm sure he'll want to see you. Would you like hot tea or coffee while you wait?"

Krystal was reminded of the first time Gabe had met with her, in the bridal suite. "No, thank you." She smiled and entered the small office, trying not to lose her carefully orchestrated calmness.

"I'm Tewa. If you need anything, please let me know." She closed the door softly, leaving Krystal to explore the interesting photographs and artifacts that decorated the walls of Gabe's tiny, secluded office.

The first thing she noticed was Vegas's decorative iron sunburst. She swelled with pride at his artistic ability. With chagrin she remembered that she had left someone of his talents repairing a stopped-up sink this morning.

On another wall there were old photos of the early days at Starfire, along with numerous Indian-designed weavings and paintings. Prominent on one wall was the bold, colorful figure of a proud, blanket-wrapped Indian woman. Closer examination revealed it was an R.C. Gorman original. Krystal eyed the painting with awe and admiration. Not many people could afford an expensive oil painting by the brash Indian artist. But Gabe Marcos could.

Abruptly he entered the room, looking muscular and trim in his black stretch ski pants and Nordic sweater of cream and rust. Krystal willed herself to calm the raging feminine instincts she felt at the sight of him.

"Sorry to keep you waiting, Krystal. Today has been one of those days—two injuries on the slopes, one a broken leg. Now the governor is bringing a small group of friends up tomorrow for the holidays and he wants private catering. Of course, one of our cooks just quit." Gabe heaved himself behind the big mahogany desk and began sifting through a stack of papers without even looking up at her.

Krystal began weakly. "I'm sorry to bother you, Gabe. But I feel that this deserves to be said, even at the expense of our valuable time."

He sighed and lifted his penetrating eyes to her. "What is it?" There was impatience in his tone.

She took a deep, calming breath. "I—I came to say I'm sorry about the other night. We had a lovely evening together, and I hated to part with such bad feelings between us."

"Not good for business, is it, Krystal?"

Her green eyes snapped angrily. "Damnit, Gabe, that's not it at all! I'm upset to know that if you can't take me to bed, you'll leave angry."

"Hell, Krystal, you know that's not the problem!"

"Then what is it, Gabe? I don't know what's wrong

with me. I find myself apologizing for going to bed with you, then apologizing for not going!"

His angular countenance cracked into a devilish grin. "Any regrets, Krystal?"

"Nope." She matched his smile.

"Me either! How would you like to look around Starfire? I need to check on a few things along the way."

"I'd love it, if you have time for me."

He rose with a smile. "I always have time for you, Krystal."

With effort she kept a businesslike attitude as they toured his small ski lodge. Compared to her quiet, deserted complex, this place was a hub of activity and fun. The early holiday snows had brought hundreds of skiers to Starfire. It was indeed good for business.

The lobby of the main lodge was a study in muted colors and shapes, all designed to lend an air of relaxation after a day of skiing. Running sofas in camel and rust wound around circular fireplaces and rested against walls of native wood paneling. And yet the appeal and warmth of the interior did not in any way detract from the glorious beauty of the Sangre de Cristo Mountains visible through multiwindowed walls.

They toured the convention facilities, then walked through the snack shop. In the cafeteria Gabe disappeared into the kitchen for a few minutes. He returned with a smile of relief. "Thank God, Delores will work overtime and cover the morning shift. I had visions of me flipping pancakes at six in the morning!"

Krystal laughed. "Oh, sure! I can just picture that!"

He opened the door and led her out. "For your information, I've done it! Of course, the situation was an emergency, but I do fix a mean pancake when I have to!"

"I'm sure you can do just about anything you have to, Gabe."

"You're right! Now on to one of the favorite haunts up here—the gift shop!"

"Talk about your basic tourist trap!" Krystal teased as they strolled through the isles of stacked items.

Gabe shrugged. "It's mostly scarves, toboggans, heavy socks, sweat shirts and coffee mugs with Starfire on them."

"Still . . ." she scoffed, raising a scarf with the word "Starfire" imprinted over mountain peaks. "This is the work of local artisans? Why, it's imported! Shame on you, Gabe Marcos!"

"You're right; it's tacky." He rolled his eyes comically, then caught her arm and pulled her ear close to his mouth. "But it sells!"

"Opportunist!" Krystal snapped testily.

He shook his head in mock seriousness. "Entrepreneur! How about a little trip up the mountain? I have visions of us having lunch there. The view from the top is spectacular."

Krystal responded with enthusiasm. "Sounds wonderful! Do you have a restaurant up there?" She glanced up at the ragged peaks.

"No. Not yet, anyway. Afterward we can ski down."

Her head swiveled quickly and she started to do some mental backpedaling. "Oh, Gabe, I'd love to, but I didn't bring my skis." How could she tell him what a poor skier she was? Here she was suggesting a merger with a ski resort owner and she couldn't even do a stem christy! Water ballet was more to her liking. In a heated pool!

He didn't even consider her dissent. "We can fix you up in our ski shop. Everything you need."

"I—uh, didn't wear heavy socks. And my feet always freeze on the slopes."

"We have those, too. Printed with 'Starfire.'" He grinned teasingly.

"As you can see, Gabe, I just wore my jeans today, and they aren't waterproof. Sometimes I can't stay on my feet when I ski."

"We'll spray them with waterproofing," he offered. "What's wrong, Krystal? Trying to get out of skiing?"

"Oh, no!" she lied. "It's just that I don't ski very well. I'm sure you don't want to bother with me. I'm very slow."

"So am I. Pulled a hamstring, remember? I'll have to take it easy. With you."

"Don't say I didn't warn you!" Krystal smiled bravely in defeat and followed Gabe into the ski shop.

Before long they were properly outfitted, and Krystal clogged along in clumsy ski boots. Gamely she shouldered her skis and headed for the ski-lift line. Gabe helped her snap the long slats onto her feet and land safely in the chair as it automatically came around. Now her only problem was getting off the damn thing in one piece!

Riding the ski lift was an absolute delight. Krystal felt a sense of soaring as they rose above the treetops with ski-weighted feet dangling. She was a snowbird, skimming the mountains' beauty, hoping for the future. But snowbirds were seasonal and temporary. Would she fall into that category by the end of the ski season? Fervently she hoped not.

She turned her rosy-cheeked, windblown face to Gabe and cast him an eager smile. This was the part she loved, going up the mountain in the chair lift. All too soon she would be demonstrating her clumsiness on the downhill run.

Gabe gazed woodenly over the land. He exhibited none of the touristy thrill Krystal still felt at the sight of the snow-covered terrain. His features were dark and serious, his thoughts hidden behind a slight scowl of black brows and jutting jaw. Those blue eyes were masked, seeking certain unseen spots in the landscape below.

An ominous feeling grew within Krystal, and she wondered what she was doing here with this man. What made her think she could do business with him? Perhaps she should just listen to Jason and hold out until the offer to buy was right!

"There," Gabe directed stiffly, pointing to the downward-sloping land. "That's the western edge of your property."

Krystal craned her head to examine the area. "How can you tell? It all looks just the same. Is it marked?"

Gabe gave her a brief, harsh stare, then answered coldly, "I just know."

Krystal had no more time to ponder his grave expression. The moment of truth was at hand as the chair lift slowed just enough to spit out its skiers at the top. Her panic mounted as she remembered the embarrassing tumbles she usually took going down the short exit ramp.

Miraculously, though, that embarrassment was avoided. As if he were reading Krystal's mind, Gabe grasped her arm firmly and pulled her along with him, forcing her to stay upright on her unsteady feet. She gave him a shaky but grateful smile as they glided smoothly down the off ramp and out of the path of the next skiers who were following close behind.

"Thanks, Gabe. As you can see, I'm not very steady on

these things. I did want to see the mountain and the view from the top. And you're right—it's spectacular. Now maybe we should just take the ski lift back down. That's more my style," she admitted with a nervous laugh.

"Don't be silly, Krystal. We're up here now, and we're going to ski down. You can manage it. And there are more beautiful views I'd like to show you. Then there's the lunch I promised." He led the way to one of the trails.

Krystal followed reluctantly. "Lunch? But where, Gabe?"

"You'll see," he assured her. "Come on." At that moment she noticed a small backpack across his shoulders that she had been too preoccupied to see before.

They did their own slow version of zigzagging down the trail, with Gabe waiting patiently for Krystal around every bend. Occasionally he veered off the main trail to lead her through ponderosa pines to a breathtaking view of jagged mountain peaks and deep gorges. All of it was his property, all belonging to this powerful man with whom she foolishly hoped to merge her unproven and untested business. It was insane!

And yet what could Gabe do with those mountain peaks and deep gorges but look at them? She was the one with the only property available for a reasonable road. Plus she had the opportunity for off-season trade with the health spa. She had as much right to establish a business up here as he did, birthright or no birthright!

"You hungry?" He interrupted her thoughts.

"Starved! What do you suggest?" She spread her hand to encompass the pine branches above and snow below.

"How about a picnic?" He aimed for a sunny area near a stand of bare-branched silver aspens.

Krystal followed and unlatched her skis. She watched,

amused, as Gabe began to unload the backpack. He first spread a small tarp just big enough for the two of them, then unpacked a long, skinny loaf of French bread and a round of cheese.

He motioned to her and quipped, "We cannot live on bread and cheese alone. We must have wine!" With a flourish he brandished a small bottle of wine and two plastic wineglasses.

Krystal kneeled beside him on the tarp, laughing. "This is one for the records! A picnic in the snow under the aspens! It's beautiful!" She almost added, With the renowned Gabe Marcos! but decided against it.

He handed her the two small, collapsible glasses and applied the corkscrew to the wine bottle. The cork popped loudly, creating a small echo in their quiet world. The sights and sounds and clean smell of snow on pine trees reeked of romance. Krystal wasn't blind to the ruse. But she wasn't an icicle, either. She could enjoy a little romance. Besides, the wine would warm her . . . though it wasn't really cold at all.

Filling the glasses, Gabe smiled with satisfaction. "I'm thinking about building a restaurant right here on this spot, Krystal. Don't you think it would be nice? I can picture it cantilevered right on the edge of the cliff, with glass walls that allow a fantastic view of the entire valley," he explained, pointing.

"Sounds spectacular, Gabe," Krystal agreed. "Also ambitious and expensive. It would probably cost a fortune to build it."

He shrugged his shoulders. "It wouldn't be cheap. But it's something I want to do. Depends on how business improves during the next couple of winters. If they're all like this one, with early snow, there'll be no problem." He sliced the cheese into small wedges and handed her one.

"If you would consider my offer, perhaps we could build a profitable business that would be year-round." Her eyes caught his with a twinkle as she nibbled the cheese. "And that would allow you to build the restaurant sooner."

"You don't give up, do you?" he commented as he tore a hunk of bread from the loaf.

"Gabe, you know it's what I want—need. Why can't you understand that it would help us both? I thought that was what this excursion was all about—preliminary business," she explained with an outstretched hand.

Gabe caught her hand and planted a slow kiss in the palm. He pulled gently until she was arousingly close to him. "No, *mi joyalita,* this is what it's all about," he said huskily just before his lips covered hers in a warm kiss.

As she felt the first explorations of his moist tongue edging against her lips, Krystal struggled against her own weak will.

One hand clutched the half-full glass of Chablis while the other spread protestingly against his chest. At her touch, he leaned closer, as if relishing it. She pushed harder, feeling the tautness of his firm, unyielding chest beneath her fingers. His energy overwhelmed her once again, and she felt herself drawn into it, closer and closer to him.

"No—" Her voice was a muffled sound.

"Yes," he responded, clearer. His lips moved sensuously along her jawline to her neck, emitting sweet whispers against her skin.

Krystal's hand slid to Gabe's shoulder, seeking his neck. The muscles were strained, the skin warm. And the warmth spread through her until the fight in her was quelled. Her mind fought it, but her body refused to obey. Perhaps . . . this one kiss. Only one kiss!

As Gabe pressed closer, Krystal eased backward until, inevitably, she was braced by something solid. The tarp! She had manuevered herself—or had she been manuevered—to the tarp and was now lying flat with nowhere to go and nothing to do but enjoy Gabe's kiss from above her.

His solid chest propelled against her, reminding her of another time when he had hovered above her. With a low, purring moan Krystal writhed beneath him, and Gabe braced himself, decreasing the pressure. But the kisses continued. His lips were sensitive and gentle, not tight and demanding. His tongue tickled the corners of her mouth until she admitted his intrusion. She tasted his sweet moisture, allowing his masculine exploration. Suddenly she realized that as his tongue roamed, so did his hand! One tender nipple rose sharply to eager firmness at his gentle squeezing, and she became acutely aware of his warm hand cupping a breast under her sweater.

How could that have happened so quickly? And without her knowing? Was it that she was so enthralled, so absolutely mesmerized by Gabe's kiss that she hadn't felt his touch until her body was responding so willingly? Oh, how could I? Krystal struggled against the magic.

Her lips moved against his, murmuring with effort, "Gabe, don't—" She felt like a schoolgirl suddenly instead of a woman fighting her own feminine responses. "Oh . . ." It was more an expression of feeling than protest.

Gabe raised his head above hers, his blue eyes passion dark. As he gazed deeply into her eyes, his hand switched its gentle persuasion to her other breast. "Krystal, you're so soft and warm. Is it any wonder I want you? And you want me, too. Your body tells me so." His voice was a thick rasp, and he lowered his head to kiss her earlobe and neck.

"Gabe, this is not why we came here! Not why I came, anyway. Please don't touch me like that!" Her voice was a strained whisper as the beginnings of desire surged through her limbs. Her flesh sizzled wherever he touched, and the rest of her longed to be free of the cumbersome ski clothes and against his virile warmth.

He paused to gaze at her through heavy-lidded eyes. "Then why are you here?"

"Why, to tour your property and to—to talk about our business," she sputtered.

"Oh no, Krystal. That's not why you came back. You know why . . ." His words faded as his lips claimed hers again.

And she knew why! Oh God, she couldn't bear the thought of not tasting his kiss again or feeling his touch. No matter what she said, that was the real, shameless truth! Her aching arms slid to his shoulders, and yearning fingers entwined in his dark hair as Krystal allowed herself to enjoy his kiss. Now that he knew, and it had been revealed, she felt the freedom to relent, to let down her defenses for a moment and give in to her feminine desires, to respond freely to the magic that Gabe Marcos conjured.

As the kiss deepened, Gabe's tongue plunged into her sweet depths, meeting no resistance. She was eager and inviting in his arms, once again creating feelings in him that he had never felt before he met her. It wasn't just the desire that swelled within him, but other emotions that surfaced confusingly.

Perhaps it was her air of innocence, her vulnerability to the pain he knew she had endured. He was overwhelmed with instincts of protectiveness he had never felt for anyone else. There was a strong wish to isolate her from the possibility of further anguish. He wanted to make her happy, to see her flash of a smile more often. He wanted her for himself alone. *Por Dios!* What was he thinking?

Gabe wrenched himself from their embrace with a low moan. "This—this is not the time or place, Krystal."

She lay very still, her eyes glowing with warm desire for this man who hovered on his elbow near her. "You're right, Gabe."

He trailed a finger along her cheek and down to the wildly pulsing hollow of her throat, exactly where his kisses had blazed only minutes ago. "We'll go back to my cabin. It's not far from here."

Realization clicked in Krystal's desire-drugged brain. Her hand covered his against the wild beating of her heart. "Oh, Gabe, you know I want you, too. But I—I need some time to sort things out first." It was the truth, for once. She wanted to go with him, but the risks involved weighed heavily on her conscience.

Gabe looked at her, lying so tantalizingly near him, knowing he could probably persuade her if he really tried. But did he want it to be that way? Maybe he, too, needed to sort out some things. Shifting from her, he poured himself another glass of wine. The slight trembling of his hands was imperceptible to her as he tilted his head back and gulped the entire contents of the small glass. He gazed at distant peaks and heaved a long breath. "All right, Krystal. Whenever you're ready."

Miserably Krystal's eyes traveled from the strained cords of his neck to the chest that had pressed so firmly against her to his flat abdomen. Inadvertently she noted the masculine bulge beneath his tight stretch pants. She sat up quickly, turning her eyes away. One kiss! Only one kiss and he was aroused! Oh, God! Krystal lifted her face gratefully to a sudden cool breeze that rustled pine needles and sent snow sprinkling to the ground nearby.

"Krystal, don't be embarrassed by what you do to me. You feel it, too, don't you?" His voice was soft.

She met his honest, piercing eyes and tried to turn away, to deny his claim.

Gabe's hand caught her chin. "Well, you do, don't you? Or am I imagining your reactions?"

Unable to lie, she gulped. "No—I mean, yes. I just need a little time."

"Your eyes tell me now is the time."

"No! I—can't!"

"Why, Krystal, are you fighting this?"

"Gabe, I—I'm afraid of this relationship. Can't you see how our personal life is affecting our business?" She felt a mounting panic at the prospect of losing control again.

"Oh, yes," he murmured, his finger caressing the top of her hand. "But it's magic, Krystal."

"Please—don't say that," she murmured, wanting to deny its truth.

"Afraid? Of more pain?" He knew what she meant, but could he promise not to hurt her again? Right now he wasn't sure.

She lowered her head and nodded.

He lifted her chin and answered her honestly. "I can only promise you this now, Krystal. Whatever happens between us will not interfere in our business."

Her emerald eyes lifted to his blue ones. "Will it help?"

His sharp eyes cut into her as he answered honestly, "No! Business is business and stands on its own merits."

"Good." She smiled, somewhat relieved. "That's exactly how I feel." From the beginning she had prayed that their personal relationship wouldn't ruin the future. She hoped he meant it.

He shifted and kissed her nose. "And now I have something special for you. We must finish this picnic and get back down the mountain."

"What now?" Krystal smiled and sipped her wine. This man was full of surprises.

Digging into the backpack, he pulled out a small plastic container. "Hope you like strawberries." He walked about twenty feet away through the snow, then bent and scooped into the white powder. He returned, a devilish smile playing on his lips, to show her the dish he had prepared.

There a bowl of huge red strawberries lay nestled in a bed of whitest snow. He picked a large berry and motioned for her to open her mouth.

"Strawberries?" she gasped. "At this time of year? Where in the world did you get them? They're huge and—"

Before she had time to finish, he popped the berry into her mouth. The sweet juice mingled with the cold snow, forming a creamy mixture that was sumptuous. Krystal laughed delightedly but held up her hand to slow him down as he leaned toward her with another snowy berry. "Hold it! I can feed myself, Gabe!"

But he held the bowl just out of her reach. "Oh, no you don't! That's half the fun. Feeding you. Seeing you smile," he murmured gently.

"Then it's only fair to let me enjoy half the fun!" She laughed and chose a berry topped with snow. Eagerly she popped it into Gabe's mouth, giggling as juice dribbled at the corners. Oh, how she wanted to kiss his mouth again. Just being close, watching him, having fun with him, brought forth deep feelings that she had been able to suppress until now. She fought the urge to be in his arms, to enjoy his pleasures, to go back to the cabin with him.

They finished the strawberries and another glass of wine. Although neither said it, they knew this delightful picnic had to end. Reluctantly, quietly, they gathered the picnic supplies and piled them into the backpack. They both had work to do this day.

Gabe helped her snap her skis back in place, and they were once again on the main trail, skiing down the mountain. Krystal struggled to keep up with Gabe. She held her breath on every curve, pressed her lips together in deep concentration to keep her knees bent and skis parallel. There was no time to consider Gabe's kisses. That would come later. Right now all she could think of was getting down this damn mountain in one piece!

As Krystal picked up speed, she tried to slow her pace by veeing her skis. Lesson number one: Keep skis parallel. Lesson number two: Make a wedge with your skis to stay in control! But her weak leg, once broken on a snowy trail such as this, gave way. She zipped, out of control, faster, wilder, over and over!

Krystal's world turned upside down. She felt herself tumbling in the cold, wet snow, the act blurred as if in slow motion. She was struck by sharp sticks, scratched by branches. It happened so fast, she wasn't even aware of the scared yelp she uttered as the rapid descent began. By the time she stopped rolling, she was only cognizant of the severe pain in her right knee and the cold chill that surged through her body. A low moan escaped from thin lips.

Krystal stared, dazed, at the blue sky, obscured by green branches, confused by intense blue eyes. Gabe's eyes! Maybe it was just her imagination. Things were still spinning! No, she was awake, because she felt pain. Hands roamed her body, pressing, lifting, bending. It was only when they reached her knee that she writhed in pain, alert to sudden, severe agony.

"Easy, now. Take it easy, Krystal." It was Gabe's voice, soothing; Gabe's form hovering over her; Gabe's hands inspecting her.

"I'm—I'm okay," she mumbled. "Help me up."

"Let me see you move this leg," he ordered.

"Oooh," she groaned as she obeyed. "I can move. It just hurts like hell. If you'll help me, I can get out of this wet snow. I'm—I'm cold."

Gabe hunched back in a stooping position, examining her face. "I think you're all right. It isn't broken or you couldn't move it at all. At least I don't think so. Would you like me to call the paramedics? They have a stretcher."

"Oh, no! That's not necessary, Gabe. I'll be fine. I'm just wet. And cold. Just give me a hand." Krystal pressed her lips together grimly, then struggled to her feet.

A firm hand steadied her and a strong arm braced her back. Krystal was allowed only one limping step before Gabe halted her. He unsnapped her heavy ski boots and, lifting her right out of them, swept her up in his arms. Leaving his own skis in the snow next to her skis and boots, he moved with surprising swiftness through the pines.

Krystal clung to his powerful shoulders and nestled in his secure arms, leaning gratefully against his firm chest. There was a sureness about his step, and Krystal entrusted herself to him. She closed her eyes against engulfing dizziness and the sudden wave of nausea that swept over her.

"Oh, God, Gabe! I feel awful!" She buried her face against his shoulder.

"Your knee? Does it hurt the way I'm carrying you?"

"No," she muttered through clenched, chattering teeth. "I just—it's my head, my stomach. Oooh! I may be sick!"

"We're almost there. Just hang in there, Krystal. It won't be long now." He continued a steady stream of words as Krystal drifted dizzily through the woods in his arms. *In Gabe's arms.*

She roused from her secure, dreamlike world when she felt herself deposited somewhere and heard his firm voice demanding that Rita be sent to his cabin. *His cabin?* Krystal sat upright and tried to look around. The faintly familiar room moved in a dizzying circle before her eyes, the elements merging in a blur of rusts and browns.

"Oooh, my head!" She clutched her aching skull and slumped back on the pillow. "Gabe? Gabe! Where am I?"

"Don't worry, *querida.*" His soothing tone reassured her. "This will help." A cool cloth was clamped on her forehead, and masculine fingers stroked her cheeks and neck. "Take it easy. Rita will be here soon."

The next thing Krystal recalled in the blur of events was someone hurting her leg. "Gabe?" She moaned herself awake, then gazed stunned and embarrassed into two faces. One was a woman's. Rita? Then Gabe, his blue eyes intense and worried. The beam of a flashlight pierced each eye, blinding and confusing her. Why were they bothering her eyes? It was the knee that hurt. Oh God, did it hurt!

A strange feminine voice penetrated Krystal's fog. "The knee is just sprained, Gabe. The dizziness and nausea are from a blow to her head. When she rolled she must have hit a stone. Here is the bruise. See?"

"Will she be all right?" It was Gabe's rumbling voice.

"Sure. But she needs complete rest, and no more pressure on that knee. Don't let her put weight on it for several days."

Days? Even in her muddled state Krystal realized that Christmas was only two days away.

With images of flickering candles and gaily decorated Christmas trees dancing in her head, Krystal dozed. The marvelous aroma of pine needles filled her nostrils. It felt so good to lie very, very still. If she didn't move a thing, or open her eyes, or turn her head, or bend her leg, there was no pain. And it was so nice, she decided, not to ever, ever move again. She would just remain here forever . . . wherever she was . . .

"Gabe?" Krystal fought her way out of the fog that enshrouded her. "Gabe!" Was he still there? Should she risk pain and open her eyes?

From somewhere in the darkness his voice consoled her. "Yes, yes, *mi querida.* I'm here."

"Where—where am I?"

"You're safe, Krystal. You're in my cabin. I'll take care of you." His voice vibrated warmly through her. It was a secure feeling. "Don't worry. Just rest."

"Gabe, don't leave me . . ." She felt like she was sinking into a tunnel. Even her own voice sounded hollow.

"I won't leave you, *mi joyalita.*"

Krystal drifted away, as if it were the most natural thing in the world to be in Gabe's cabin and for him to be taking care of her. She was wrapped in secure comfort throughout the day and night, savoring the pine-filled fragrance of her warm haven, free of pain, in Gabe's arms, where she belonged.

CHAPTER SIX

Krystal woke to the sound of a man's voice and the rich aroma of coffee brewing. The pine fragrance was gone. So was the pain. Maybe it was safe to open her eyes. Hesitantly she squinted, one eye at a time. The bed, the room, the sounds were totally unfamiliar to her. For a brief, panicky moment she didn't know where she was. Her eyes settled alarmingly on the broad back of a man who sat on the edge of the other side of her bed. Her bed? *Whose* bed?

Then she remembered. The man was Gabe Marcos. And this was Gabe's bed! Oh God, she should remember that!

Krystal struggled to sit up, but that prompted pain and dizziness. She slumped against the pillow and tried to get his attention. "Gabe! What happened? Why am I here?" Immediately visions of the accident blurred in her mind. The picnic in the snow and skiing and . . . the fall! Gabe was there, carrying her . . . where? Here? After that the flashes were brief and vague.

Gabe kept his back turned but held up his hand to hush her. In a moment he cradled the phone and turned to Krystal with a smile. "Well, it's about time you opened those beautiful green eyes to face the world! How do you feel this morning?" He walked around the bed and sat on the edge, very near where she lay. *His* bed!

Krystal blinked at his words. Her hand went involuntarily to her head. "Morning? Is it still morning? The accident left me a little fuzzy."

He laughed. "It's still morning for another couple of hours. Did you sleep well last night? How's your head?"

Her eyes opened wider as she stared up at him. "Last night? Oh Gabe, do you mean that I spent the night here?"

"Right here," he affirmed with a nod, apparently amused at her unrest. It gave him pleasure to tell her, "You were perfectly safe and warm in my arms."

"In your arms? Last night?" She stared at him, open-mouthed, trying to recall everything . . . anything.

"You keep repeating what I say. Are you sure you're all right, Krystal?" His hands framed her face, examining her for a temperature or broken bones. Light caresses ranged the length of her neck, his fingertips stroking either side, then spreading over her bare shoulders.

Bare shoulders? Suddenly Krystal realized that all she wore was a thin camisole and her brief bikini panties! "Gabe! My clothes?" she sputtered.

"Not to worry. They're drying. I couldn't very well tuck you into bed—my bed—with all those wet clothes on, could I? Anyway, nothing binding, remember? First aid rule number one."

"So you conveniently took care of them! Well, thank you, but I'll need them back! Right now! I want to get dressed!" His masculine arrogance was infuriating.

"Why do you need to get dressed? You aren't going anywhere!" He viewed her with a pleased smile. She was right where he wanted her.

"Oh, yes I am! I'm going home!"

"Oh, no you aren't! You're staying right here! Doctor's orders!"

"Doctor? What doctor?" She *was* fuzzy!

"Actually I had Rita, my chief medic, check you over. She assured me the knee wasn't broken, just twisted. And she gave me instructions not to let you put any weight on it for several days."

"Days? Tomorrow is Christmas!" Krystal whimpered miserably. She was supposed to be in Albuquerque with Jason's family. "I shouldn't be here today! It's Christmas Eve!"

"Hmmm, so it is. Well, I can't think of a better place for you to be. I must admit I've been trying to think of an ingenious way to get you into my bed, but it looks like you solved that little problem by yourself!" The mischievous gleam in his eyes was just too much for her.

"At least you're damned honest about your intentions!" Krystal threw a pillow at him, which he easily dodged.

His fingers swiftly encased her wrists, halting her aggression. "Easy, now. I've already called Vegas to tell him where you are. He requested some time off, and I said I'd check with the boss and get back with him later today. He reported that the sink was fixed and draining properly."

She was caught, literally trapped. "But Gabe, I can't just stay here. It's Christmas. Please take me back home."

"Who would take care of you there?" he asked sensibly as his thumbs made maddening circles on her inner wrists. "Vegas will probably be leaving for Christmas. Even if he stayed, I'm sure he couldn't take care of you. Not like I can."

"And you can?" she asked indignantly, attempting to sit again. "You're running a ski resort, during the busiest season of the year! And the busiest holiday! I can't ask you to—"

His hands caressed her shoulders as he pushed her firmly back down on the pillow. "The difference is that I have plenty of help. Delores is sending some soup over for lunch. Don't worry about a thing, Krystal. You are safe in my hands. If I can spend the entire night holding you and doing nothing else, I can certainly take care of a simple sprained knee."

"Gabe! You were in here with me?" Her question was soft and had a little-girl quality. "In this bed?"

"Right in here," he teased, slipping one hand under the covers to tickle her waist. "I felt responsible for keeping you warm. Did I do a good job?"

"I—I guess so. I wasn't cold." She blushed just thinking of being curled up next to Gabe Marcos all night. And she didn't even remember it!

His lips were dangerously close to hers. "I must admit, it was one of the hardest things I've ever done, just holding you and not loving you." When he finished talking, his lips closed the remaining gap between them.

His kiss was gentle and persuasive, with desire obvious in the heated exchange. His fresh scent accosted her nostrils, and Krystal breathed deeply of the outdoors fragrance. *Pine trees!* It was him! All night!

"You—you just held me? All night? And nothing else? They'd never believe me!" She teased with a grin when he raised his head.

"You won't have a chance to tell them, because I'm not going to let you go now. Not unless you want to tell all a few days from now." It was a threat, a promise of what was to happen between them. Admittedly Krystal was thrilled at the prospect.

"I'm not the tattling type," she purred. The mood between them was changing. He had shown compassion and taken care of her. Perhaps he really cared.

"Good. I'm not the holding type. I prefer more action."

His kisses trailed over her face while she tried to think straight.

"Why did you bother with me? Why didn't you send me to the hospital?"

"Because you needed me, Krystal. You were in pain and so helpless. I guess I wanted you here with me. I wanted to think I was the only one who could help you."

"Gabe Marcos, you're—amazing," she marveled, meeting his waiting lips with a welcoming kiss. This one was more meaningful, more passionate.

"Wait till later before you decide," he instructed as his lips nibbled at her jawline and down the sensitive column of her neck. When he kissed the throbbing hollow of her throat, he raised his passion-darkened eyes, muttering teasingly, "Now that's what I like—a responsive woman. Last night you were no fun at all!"

"Gabe!" Krystal squirmed, wondering what had actually transpired last night.

"Don't worry, *mi joyalita.* Nothing at all happened. You slept like a babe in my arms all night. But now it's different. No one wants to sleep."

"Gabe, I don't think we should—" She gasped as his hands proved her wrong.

Pushing the covers away, he caressed her partly exposed breasts. Under the silk camisole, dark tips poised firmly at his touch. "You don't think what? Apparently your body has different ideas, *mi amor.* And I like what I see!"

His palms covered the soft mounds, kneading them skillfully as he again kissed her willing lips. A warm, roguish tongue opened her lips insistently, then swept past her teeth to plunge the dark sweetness of her mouth. His hands moved over the slick material of her camisole, and the friction brought each breast to aching firmness as his kiss deepened with strong desire.

Krystal arched to his touch in newly awakened pleasure, her arms lifting automatically to embrace his neck. Entwining slender fingers in the ebony hair at the base of his neck, she responded spiritedly to his skillful hands.

As his lips blazed their own fiery trail, he unfastened her arms from their grip on him and slipped her straps down, freeing the swelling breasts from the ecru silk encumbrance. He pinned her hands above her head on the pillow, then allowed his fingertips to sensuously stroke the length of her arms.

His eyes were dark sapphires, and he groaned with undisguised delight, as if he were about to enjoy a savory meal. Indeed his tongue encircled each rosy tip in turn, gently nibbling until Krystal thrust them firmly outward, demanding and seeking more.

Her eyes were half-open clefts of emerald, and she sucked in her breath sharply. "Gabe . . . oh, Gabe . . ."

His lips closed over each tip, pulling, exciting, demanding, until it was a hard knot in his mouth. He scraped white teeth ever so carefully over the tight buttons as his hands followed her feminine shape, tracing ribs, waist, hips. Slipping each palm under her hips, he found his way under her bikini panties to knead her rounded buttocks.

Krystal moaned softly and thrust her hips in response to his rhythmic motions. She watched his angular face soften in passion as he reverently scanned her body with his hands, celebrating her curves and responses with obvious adoration. She was amazed at her lack of embarrassment as Gabe continued his explorations of her heated femininity. It seemed so natural, so wonderful to reveal herself to him, and she delighted in the masculine arousal she could see in him. She wanted him eagerly. Her limbs ached for the burning satisfaction only Gabe could give.

In the next moment Gabe halted his heated advances with stinging abruptness. Muttering a low groan, he raked a large hand over his face and turned from her. "Krystal, this isn't fair. I am expected at the lodge, and people are coming here. We have to wait."

"Gabe, don't stop—" Krystal begged hoarsely. It was as bold a comment as she had ever made.

His eyes were heavy-lidded as he turned back to her. She was his, if he would only stay. That was what she was saying! He paused, tempted, yet hating himself for what he was about to do. She was so beautiful and eager. Oh, God, he wanted her! He hoped she would understand and wait.

"I—I can't." With a muttered oath Gabe pulled the covers over Krystal's nudity. Stiffly he rose and tried to explain. "I—we don't have time. Now is just not right. I—I'm sorry. I have to take care of some problems at the lodge. Surely you understand, Krystal. Sometimes it's unavoidable when you're the boss. I'll be back as soon as possible." The strain of interrupted passion was obvious on his face. She had to believe him.

Krystal stared at Gabe, then turned her face away in frustration. Did he feel the same agony she did? It still didn't relieve the aching disappointment. To have been brought so close to passion's promise only to be delayed was nerve shattering. But then she should have known better. It was mid-morning, and a workday for most people.

"I understand—maybe," she mumbled. Her physical

response had been so willing, so eager, that it was almost embarrassing to face him.

Gabe paced near the bed, running a hand raggedly around the back of his neck. "Krystal, I didn't intend for that kiss to go so far. Today is special, you know, and there would have been interruptions."

"Oh?" She tucked the cover demurely under her arms.

"Well, for one thing, don't forget, it's Christmas Eve. No one on my staff feels like working today. And yet we have to keep the business going." He sat beside her again and touched her hair. "Then I have a beautiful woman tucked away in my cabin. That doesn't happen often, no matter what you've heard. To top it off, she's injured. They'll be doing everything they can to 'help' today."

"All right, Gabe. There'll be time later, I suppose." She smiled, trying to understand, to forgive. However, this was Christmas, and the hopelessness of her situation was beginning to sink in. "I just can't believe I'm stuck here on Christmas, Gabe! I'm supposed to be on my way to Jason's right now!"

"Jason?" he barked.

She nodded, pouting. "My cousin and his family. They have twin boys, and we were going to have fun with Santa's visit and everything!"

"Don't worry, *mi querida,* I'll make sure Santa knows where to find you!" He leaned over her and kissed her nose affectionately.

"Thanks," she scoffed.

"Actually, it's not so bad, Krystal. You'll have plenty of company today. Delores has made some soup, and Rita's coming over now to check on your injuries. Incidentally, how's the knee?"

"I don't know. We didn't get to the knee yet!"

He rose with a hearty laugh. "I'll check it out later. And I promise to get to the knee! Until tonight you stay put! I have plans for us later, and I think you'll enjoy them. Since you're having company soon, you'd better get some clothes on. How about a nice warm shirt?"

"My clothes? Yes!"

"No, mine. Yours are being laundered. Here, this ought to do the trick." He peeled a baby blue linen shirt from his closet and tossed it to her. "No, wait! On second thought, let me." Before she could blink, he was beside her, slipping her arms into the sleeves.

With painfully slow motions he buttoned each tiny white button, allowing his hands to caress her silky skin along the way. The last button closed just below the tempting tuft of golden hair at the juncture of her long legs. He looked longingly up into her dancing green eyes. "God, I don't want to leave you!"

"Don't get any ideas," she admonished with a sly grin. "Duty calls, remember? And I'm having company soon!"

"To hell with duty! And I'll lock the doors!" He groaned just as the boards on the front porch creaked and a strong knock echoed from the door.

"There they are now! And I'm starved!" Krystal exclaimed, basking in the assurance that he would be back and she would lie in his arms tonight.

"The phone's right here. If you need anything—anything at all—just pick it up and ring Tewa, my secretary. She'll help you. You probably should call Vegas. He's waiting for your okay before he leaves. And since you won't be there . . ." Gabe smiled and sauntered to the door. "We'll have our own celebration, Krystal. And it'll be wonderful."

She nodded, feeling completely and totally overwhelmed by the power of this man. He was in charge of everything he touched, including her. Was this what it would be like if they did manage to cooperate in a business deal? Would everything go his way? Or was this actually her way? Was she right where she wanted to be, too?

During the day a steady stream of well-meaning, curious visitors kept Krystal occupied. A phone call to Jason explained her predicament, assured him she was all right and apologized about Christmas. She felt a little depressed after talking to him and being reminded of the fun and family she was missing.

Then she called Vegas, saying, "Of course, take some time off. I'll see you after New Year's. Have a merry Christmas."

The old man was relieved to hear that she was safe and grateful for the holiday. Krystal felt better after talking to him. Perhaps it was the spirit of giving someone a little happiness that boosted her. Perhaps it was just being here, waiting for Gabe to return.

She came to the conclusion that being with Gabe Marcos over Christmas wasn't so bad after all. In fact, it was an enviable position.

It was an agonizingly long time until dusk, when Krystal finally heard Gabe's Jeep roar up the secluded road and halt near the cabin. Instantly her body reacted to thoughts of intimacy with him. She felt a heart-pounding, warm tingling deep inside as she listened to him on the porch. He stomped the snow off his boots loudly and fiddled impatiently with the key.

Then he was in the house, walking across the length of the living room, calling merrily, "Hey! Anybody home? *Felizes Navidades,* Krystal! *Felizes Navidades!*"

When he finally poked his weary face through the bedroom doorway, Krystal was almost breathless in anticipation. Never had she been so eager to see anyone. Maybe it was the beginning of cabin fever. Maybe—something else.

But one look at him told her it was the man.

"There you are, my little Christmas jewel! How do you feel?"

She shrugged, marveling at her outward calm. "Okay." Should she tell him how she really felt? How her heart pounded against her breast and her palms perspired at the thought of touching him! Of him touching her! Cool down! she told herself. "Lonely," she said wistfully.

"Didn't Rita come? And Delores? And Tewa?"

"Oh, yes. They were wonderful."

Suddenly a devilish gleam lit Gabe's blue eyes. "Did Santa Claus come by? Frankly, I told him to stay the hell away! I hope you don't mind, Krystal, but I just didn't want another man here—with you. I told him I would take care of your Christmas presents myself!"

Her green eyes crinkled with glee at his spontaneity, and her laughter joined his. "Rest assured, no man has been here. Certainly not Santa!"

"Thank God! I want you all to myself!"

She shrugged her hands helplessly. "You've got me. I called Vegas. And Jason."

"Good. I brought lots of food. Mariah, my new cook, made some terrific lamb stew for tomorrow. And tamales for tonight. You know, it's a Mexican tradition to eat tamales on Christmas Eve."

"Sounds great."

He eyed her with satisfaction. "Be glad you're bundled up here, safe and warm and dry! The weather is terrible, and more snow is predicted for tonight. It's great for business, but it's damn cold out there!"

"I should be grateful I'm here—is that what you're saying?" She smiled wryly.

"You should be grateful I haven't already ravished your gorgeous body! You are so tempting there in my bed—and my shirt!"

She laughed, relieved and happy that his thoughts corresponded with her own. "I am grateful! You and your staff take very good care of injured guests, Mr. Marcos. They have kept up a steady stream of chicken soup and hot chocolate and spiced tea and books and—what else?"

"Great! As per my instructions, of course. Would you like a nice hot rum toddy?"

She nodded with pleasure. "Sounds good."

He snapped his fingers and wheeled around. "Two hot buttered rums coming right up! Anything the lady wants!"

Krystal smiled absently at the empty doorway after he disappeared. She could hear him clanking around in the kitchen. Once again Gabe Marcos was in charge. And yet it was a strange relief to accept the fact that he could handle things. In a way, she wanted to turn it all over to him—her life, her business, her love.

Love? Was it possible? How could she dream that what they shared was love or something even close to it? It was much too soon! And it was much too risky! She couldn't possibly allow herself such vulnerability.

Don't—don't even think it, she told herself. Loving Gabe Marcos would just mean more pain. And you couldn't endure any more! Don't forget why you came here to these mountains! She took a deep, determined breath. She would enjoy these next few days with Gabe, then walk away with detachment. She would not be hurt again.

Gabe appeared then to sweep her up in his arms.

"Gabe! What—"

He carried her into the rustic living room. "It's time for a change of scenery. How about having that hot toddy right in front of the fire?" Placing her gently on the sofa, he propped pillows behind her back and covered her with a beautifully woven Indian blanket.

Krystal watched, enthralled, as he bent before the stone fireplace and added logs to the dwindling flames. It crackled noisily, welcomingly, and the marvelous aroma of burning mesquite filled the room. It was a wintry, Christmasy smell, and she was suddenly very glad to be here. The sight of Gabe puttering around her, the pungent smells of the blazing wood, the sounds of Christmas songs sung in Spanish on the radio, all made her feel this was exactly where she belonged on Christmas Eve.

Gabe moved around the kitchen, humming along with the Christmas tunes on the radio. Snow fell softly on the windowpanes, piling white powder slowly on the countryside. Krystal felt particularly warm and secure, tucked away in Gabe's cabin.

Abruptly a thought occurred to her and she was impelled to ask, "What do you do about that winding road up the mountain when the weather is this bad?"

He handed her a steaming mug of something spicy and fragrant. "Bad weather? We call this good weather. Very good for business."

She sipped the drink and relished the warm sensations radiating through her insides. "It isn't very good if people can't get up that treacherous road."

His eyes pierced her sharply. "Never give up, do you, Krystal?"

She shrugged. "I just wondered. You don't have to snap my head off. I've traveled that road in good weather, and I can't imagine manuevering it in icy conditions."

Gabe shook his head and heaved himself down on a stool near the fire. His tone was tired, and he lowered his defenses briefly. "It was passable for a few hours at noon. But cars skidded all over the place this afternoon. Now it's frozen solid again and very dangerous. You're right, Krystal. It's a sonovabitch. I need that new road through your valley." He gulped the warm drink.

She smiled tightly. "Should we talk business now?"

He looked up at her quickly. "Definitely not. Pleasure before business. I want to forget it for now. My assistant is on call tonight. We can relax with no interruptions."

"Guaranteed?" She grinned.

"Guaranteed!" Gabe said emphatically, emptying his drink and setting it aside before coming to her. He kneeled beside the sofa, and those bewitching eyes captured her quietly.

Involuntarily Krystal smiled, happy to be drowning in their depths, eager to be part of him. He could see it in her face, she was sure. But for once she wasn't ashamed of revealing those feelings.

Large, tanned hands cradled her face, his thumbs measuring her cheekbones while he kissed her smiling lips with sensuous sweetness. He sipped and tasted, lightly sampling until Krystal wanted to cry and force him against her, into her. But that was not Gabe's way. Not now. He purposely savored every bite, drinking with his eyes, partaking with his lips . . . drowning her ever so slowly in desire. After waiting for him all day, it was mitigated torture.

"Ah, so sweet and warm," he murmured between nibbles. "I've been thinking about this moment—and you—all day."

She dared to open her eyes and meet his, admitting, "Me, too. It's been awful here without you, Gabe. I looked at that empty bed where you sleep, the pillow where you lay your head, and I wished you were there beside me."

"Not nearly as much as I wanted to be there. I resented working today knowing you were here, in my cabin, in my bed—waiting for me. I was afraid you would leave." His hands slid to her shoulders and down the length of her arms slowly.

"I considered it, Gabe," she allowed honestly. "But something—kept me here."

"Your injured knee, obviously." He smiled.

"No, not the knee. I wanted to stay. Wanted you to return to me." Krystal's hands crept around his neck, her fingers burrowing possessively in his ebony hair.

"I'm yours all night and all day, *mi amor.* You won't be able to pry me from your arms."

"Sounds wonderful!" She smiled happily. "I want you near me, Gabe, holding me all night, like you did last night. But this time I want to remember everything. And have a part in it."

An expression of mock pain crossed his face. "Don't remind me of those long, hard hours. Just touching you, I was in agony all night but could do nothing for relief. Holding you isn't enough, Krystal. I want all of you. I want to make love to you."

"You don't have to ask," she murmured ardently. "Can't you tell I want you, too?"

“Oh, God, Krystal—” His lips devoured her vigorously, almost painfully. The kiss deepened, and Krystal’s lips opened to his thrusting tongue. She met it with her own warm, eager temptation.

Gabe’s eyes were dark sapphires when he raised his head from her bruised lips. “*Mi amor* . . . let me see you.” His fingers deftly unbuttoned the shirt and folded it back from her creamy flesh with slow reverence. His eyes feasted on her delicate skin, lighting with obvious appreciation of what he beheld. Tonight she was all his! Just looking at her, thinking about what was to come, aroused him.

His voice was a rough rumble. “What a beautiful woman you are, Krystal. So fair and—touchable.” His hands framed either side of her breasts, pushing them gently together. Her light skin paled beside his darkness as he lowered his head to her.

Krystal gasped audibly at the first touch of his warm, pink tongue on her quivering breasts. He circled their creamy fullness, homing in on his target until his lips closed gratefully on the strawberry-color tips, tasting their fresh ripeness. She arched against his mouth, pushing the swollen mounds to further pleasure. When he had taken his fill of them, savoring every morsel, his kisses lavished her damp cleavage, then nibbled their way to her navel. The continued exploration of his darting tongue rendered her helpless, and Krystal purred with undisguised joy.

“I—I think it’s time to go back to bed,” he muttered raggedly.

“Yes—yes,” she begged, letting the shirt fall from her while clutching his shoulders.

He swung her up easily into his arms and strode across the room. Krystal adored the erotic rubbing of his sweater against her bare breasts. There was something about the way Gabe treated her, cherished her when he touched her, that let all inhibitions drop away. She wanted to please him, to make him laugh, to give him ultimate pleasure. He laid her gently on the bed, as one would place an open tray of fragile porcelain, admiring her exquisite curves with his eyes.

She lay in eager anticipation while he discarded his clothes with urgent, shaky hands. He stripped his sweater over his head, revealing a ginger-colored, smooth chest and arm muscles. Boots thudded against the floor, and the slide of his zipper assured her his slacks would soon join them.

Then he faced her, his darkly exotic body completely divulged. He exuded a masculine strength, almost a savagery, that was glorified by his nude body. She had not forgotten this image of him. This magnificent male vision was one she would always remember and cherish.

Gabe stood for a moment, gazing at Krystal like a sleek animal stalking his prey. The only difference was that she was here by choice. She was no quarry, caught against her will. She wanted him, too.

She shivered in spite of herself. Yet she had the distinct feeling that whatever was happening between them tonight was grand and wonderful. There was nothing about this act that wasn't right. She knew she belonged with Gabe Marcos.

With a receptive smile, she opened her arms to him.

Carefully he eased against her, setting the length of her ablaze with his fiery skin. The rounded smoothness of his chest lingered against her breasts until her knotted tips wantonly matched his.

"Oh, Gabe, don't stop—never stop!"

"No, *mi amor,* not this time. There'll be no stopping," he said hoarsely.

His firm stomach flattened against her soft abdomen, and his hands spanned her back to settle in firm grips on both buttocks. She arched to meet his hard strength, unyielding and increasingly forceful. His knee separated her legs and he stroked her inner thighs and touched the core of her femininity.

"Come to me, Gabe . . ."

"We must be careful not to hurt your knee."

"It's all right."

"I need you—now!" He manuevered skillfully over her aroused form, settling himself into the heart of her being.

A soft cry escaped her lips, and she realized the magnificent fullness of him. She had been too long without love. In all that time Gabe Marcos was the only man she had ever wanted, who could ever fulfill this passionate longing.

With amazing restraint he held his sharp passion in check until Krystal joined in the slow rhythm he initiated. She soon discovered the overpowering vortex of desire that can engulf two lovers, and the pace quickly increased to a whirl of ecstatic entrancement. Everything was obliterated from their minds as they sought desire's culmination. To reach the zenith together, the ultimate, seemed an unattainable goal in such a brief relationship. And yet simultaneous sounds of triumph were audible in the strains of evening, and they sealed a special, magical bond together, forever.

They slumped together, relaxed, blending their souls in the still, sweet aftermath of love. Gabe's breathing gradually returned to normal, and damp wisps of blond curls clung to Krystal's temples. Eventually she could feel him slipping from her and she grasped him, closing her femininity tightly around him. She wanted him, forever and always, to stay with her. "Don't leave me," she begged spontaneously.

"We have some special magic, Krystal," he said thickly.

"Oh, yes, yes," she said, the sounds muffled against his shoulder, kissing, tasting his fragrant skin. She had never known such spires of passion as she felt with Gabe, but whether it was magic or passion or love, she wasn't sure. Not now. She could only admit that she didn't want to leave him, didn't want to lose that desirous penetration from his body. But it was not to be, and she knew it.

He moved and shifted, nestling her against him. "Beautiful, *mi joyalita.* We move together in harmony."

"Gabe, I—I have never felt like this. Never. It seems so right. I feel as though I've known you forever." She rested against his chest, listening to the steady pounding beneath his ribs.

He chuckled and stroked the length of her arm and shoulder. "You can't claim we're strangers anymore."

She stretched up to kiss him. "No. Definitely not strangers!"

His palm caressed the length of her, then pulled the covers over them. "Let's save this heat we've generated." He turned to her, continuing to stroke and soothe, reviving her heated passions. Molding himself erotically to her curved body, he pressed against the sensitive flesh of her hips. His hands cupped her breasts, and tiny kisses emblazoned the back of her neck.

"Gabe! Again? So soon?"

His laugh generated low in his chest, and she could feel its vibrations. "It's up to you, *querida.* See what you can do about it. Touch me . . ."

Using instincts she didn't even know she had and following instructions from Gabe, Krystal created more fire than she thought was possible. "Do you like this? And this?"

As Gabe's masculinity grew beneath her fingers, he groaned with pleasure. "Ah, Krystal, you *are* a witch! You have a sorceress's touch."

"I guess I do, don't I?" She laughed delightedly, proud of her newly acquired power. "And now I will use all my powers on you!"

"That's the way I like you, Krystal. Wanting me!"

"I do! I want you—want you so much, Gabe."

They made love again, beautifully and passionately. Finally they parted long enough for a Christmas Eve celebration of spicy homemade tamales with a green olive tucked inside, accompanied by a glass of rich Burgundy. Curled nude together under the Indian blanket on the sofa before the fire, they relished each other's presence. The physical joy was joined with the emotional to create a spirit of mutual belonging.

"Gabe, if I weren't here, what would you do for Christmas?" Her finger wove a filigree of circles along his sensitive chest.

"Oh, sometimes I go to my sister's in Santa Fe and spend the holidays with her family. But I'd much rather be here with you. This is far more satisfying." His large hand rested on her hip, stroking the silky skin occasionally.

"Are you sure?" She edged his mouth with a single fingertip.

"Positive! You had to cancel your plans with Jason and his family, didn't you?" He coiled a loose strand of her hair around his finger.

She nodded, her blond hair teasing his skin. "I called

him today. He was disappointed, but understanding. Frankly, I'm right where I want to be, too."

"We'll look back on this as a special time, Krystal." He held her tighter, pressing her securely to his warmth.

"I hope so . . ." There was wistfulness in her tone, and she basked in his warmth. This was where she belonged.

"You know, maybe the Pueblos were right. The old ones say that the winter is a season to replenish the spirit. They even have a name for it: the Time of Staying Still. It's when the earth lies sleeping under the snow, building fresh strength for the renewal of spring. Sometimes we all need that. This will be our Time of Staying Still, Krystal, a time for physical healing and gathering strength for what lies ahead."

She cuddled in the strength of his arms. "You're right, Gabe. I do need this time for healing." Silently she prayed for healing of her wounded spirit as well.

"I know, Krystal." He kissed the back of her ear and buried his lips against her neck.

But did he know? Actually? He couldn't possibly know the extent of pain she felt inside. No one did.

Krystal closed her eyes, grateful for Gabe's strength, his wonderful lovemaking, his Indian philosophy. A Time of Staying Still. He couldn't know how desperately, how sadly her soul cried out for relief of the burden she alone carried. Oh yes, she needed Gabe Marcos—needed his love, his understanding, his support. She could only hope he needed her, too.

CHAPTER SEVEN

Gabe dropped the phone back into its cradle and turned to Krystal. "There, now. I've taken care of Anaya. She's bringing the kids up to ski for a few days after Christmas. I like that idea better, anyway. I love my sister and her boisterous family, but to be honest, I like them better on my own turf."

Krystal reached up lazily to trace imaginary figures on his bare chest. "How many children does she have?"

"Three—two beautiful little girls and one rascal of a boy. She and her husband felt obligated to give his family a masculine namesake. Thank God it didn't take more than three tries!"

Her finger followed his rugged jawline, marveling at the smoothness she found there. "Don't you want a namesake, Gabe? Someone to carry on the great Marcos name?"

"I don't feel obligated to populate the world for my own inflated ego! Actually I've been too busy worrying about my business and family over the years to consider kids. I guess it would be nice, but a family usually requires a wife." He opened his mouth and nipped playfully at her roving fingertips.

"Too busy trying out the field?" She pursued the shape of his lips.

Gabe raised up on one elbow and glared at her menacingly. "Look, young lady, I don't know whom you've been talking to, but I am not the Don Juan you think I am!"

She giggled and said sarcastically, "Couldn't prove it by me! Look how quickly I landed in your bed! You must have a guilty conscience. You're awfully defensive!"

"I'm just defensive of you, *mi querida.* I want to keep you happy and satisfied!" He nuzzled her earlobe beneath a golden strand of hair. "It's about to kill me, too. Hmmm, you smell nice!"

"You're keeping me very happy, *señor,*" she murmured blissfully, trying to smother the shiver that ran through her as his velvet lips stroked her bare shoulder.

His hand brushed aside the coverlet and moved sensuously down the length of her nude form. Gently he caressed her injured leg. "How's the knee this morning? The swelling seems to be gone."

"It's much better! Watch!" Proudly she flexed her leg muscle without the pain of the previous day.

"Great! A little movement in the joint! See what staying in bed will do for you? Now what you need is a little physical therapy."

"Physical therapy?" She laughed deep within her chest. "Here?"

"Sure. In the hot tub."

"Oh, wonderful! I'd love it! Let's go now!"

"Later," he mumbled as his arms enfolded her close to his warm, naked length. "Right now I'd love to love you." His lips sought her sensitive neck.

"Gabe!" She was propelled against his conspicuous arousal. "This morning?"

"Why not?" he reasoned. "Morning is a great time to make love! It's refreshing! And what an invigorating way to start the day!" He pulled the blanket back over them both and let his hand trail the curves of her entire length.

"Gabe," she whispered pensively. "This is Christmas Day."

"So? Have you sworn off sex on Christmas?"

"No." She laughed softly, her breath falling warmly on his chest. "It's just that here we both are, snowed in, practically. No families. And I can't even walk."

One long brown arm gently cradled her against his rigid masculine body. "Do you want some sympathy, Krystal? You won't get it here. Frankly, I can't think of a sweeter way to spend Christmas. Maybe together we can create some wonderful memories of our own. Just the two of us." His hand dug into the mass of golden hair that tumbled around her creamy shoulders, his kisses seeking the softly pulsating spot on her temple.

She shuddered with desire and linked her arms around his waist. "No, Gabe, I'm definitely not looking for sympathy. I just want to make sure you want me here. Honestly, I feel like I belong here. Right here in your arms."

His lips sought hers. "So do I, *querida.* You belong here with me, away from the outside world. I've never felt so sure of anything, so good . . ."

Krystal's emerald eyes darkened with yearning, and her submission was obvious even before she spoke in a broken, low tone. "Gabe—kiss me—love me—again . . ."

His solid, muscular leg hooked over hers, pinning her against his unyielding mass. "Krystal, Krystal, you are like a little blond jewel who came into my life. Your hair—it reminds me of gold." He stroked it admiringly, then combed his long, tanned fingers through its length. Its lightness contrasted sharply with Gabe's raven hair and dusky complexion.

"Your eyes are like mirrors that reflect your feelings. They flash when you're angry, and glow with desire when

I make love to you. Like now!" He kissed her half-closed lids with somber reverence. "Green eyes—I love them. And those lips! I can't stay away from them—"

As if to prove his weakness, he closed his lips sensuously over hers. His tongue darted devilishly in and out, stroking, teasing, tempting. Moist kisses then skipped over her chin and down the column of her neck, setting her skin aflame.

"Your breasts are so soft and responsive . . ." Tiny, mesmerizing kisses captivated each rounded mound, gently bringing about a satisfyingly visible response. Gabe watched with masculine pride as the rosy points deepened in color and eagerly perked to meet his provocation. They grew tight as he delighted her with his hypnotizing tongue. Krystal watched in amazement as his white teeth nipped the dark tips to button hardness.

"Oh, Gabe!" she squeaked at the sharp sensations. "Be careful!"

"Be still, *querida!*" he commanded. "I want you to relax and enjoy." He gently cupped her aching breasts with warm hands and rolled the nipples between thumb and forefinger while his lips trailed hotly over her belly, and lower.

"I'm enjoying," she rasped thickly. "But relaxing is something else. Oh, Gabe . . ."

Grasping her thighs, he moved them so he could kiss the sensitive inner flesh. "You're so responsive to me here . . . and here . . ."

"Only to you, Gabe," she confided. "Only you . . ."

Krystal purred softly, willing to comply and eager for Gabe's every pleasure. Oh yes, this was a Christmas she would long remember. There had never been another like it!

His long fingers spread over her flat abdomen, then boldly lower to her soft feminine warmth. Each electrifying kiss and touch elicited mellow moans of pleasure from her throat as spirals of ever-increasing desire spread through her limbs.

"Ohhh, Gabe, don't wait . . ."

"Don't rush it, *mi amor* . . . relax and enjoy." Skillfully he brought her to the brink of wildfire, then assuaged her flames with tempered, soothing kisses. Then again . . . and again, until Krystal begged for the fulfillment only Gabe's virile force could give.

"Now! Please, Gabe—" She grasped his shoulders, pulling him urgently to her.

"Slow and easy, Krystal. I want you to enjoy this as much as I do." His nibbling kisses were driving her crazy.

"Gabe—" She buried her hands in his dark hair as his lips made their way erotically up the resilient, aroused length of her body.

"You are so sweet, *mi joyalita* . . ." Obligingly he moved over her, taunting her with his suppliant potency.

Krystal moaned with denied satisfaction and arched to meet his poised strength. His kiss claimed her already parted lips. His tongue plunged her honeyed depths, setting in motion the rhythm that she matched with her hips. With frantic, vigorous thrusting, she surged against him, finally forcing him into her warmth with impatient fervor. The impact was wild and wonderful, each reaching that ecstatic peak in a blaze of throbbing energy. Her muffled cry of rapture pierced the silver enchantment of the morning as their passion exploded in multiple bursts of spiraling peaks. Krystal wished the sensations would never end as she soared to new heights of pleasure.

Now and forever, she was his and only his. She clung

fervently to this man who loved her so completely, her fingers digging into his taut buttocks, attempting to press him even more into her every cell, her heart, her life.

They lay merged together in the ultimate finale of love for long, semidrugged minutes, breathless and satiated.

Finally a voice rumbled from deep within him. "Ah, *mi joyalita navidad . . . Felizes Navidades,* Krystal."

She sighed with sublime happiness. "Merry Christmas, Gabe. *Felizes Navidades.*" Krystal wrapped one leg possessively around him and ran slender fingers down the column of his spine, pressing on the lower part of his strong back. He moved within her, and she sighed with the ultimate feeling of satisfaction. He was hers, if only for the moment.

"Ah, *magnífica . . .*"

"Gabe," she murmured against his neck. "You are the only one I have ever responded to like this."

"I find that hard to believe, *querida.* You were married . . ."

"It was never like this. And there has been no one else. I swear it."

"Oh, God . . ." He nuzzled her neck. Spontaneously he moved again, still inside her. "You and I create something special together, Krystal. I feel like we were always meant to be like this. Together. You're so warm and wonderful, so good."

"I didn't know it could be so wonderful, Gabe."

He cradled her beside him. "After breakfast I have to check on things at the lodge. Then, around one or two, I'll be back. We'll try the hot tub then."

She raked her fingernails tantalizingly along his back. "I can hardly wait."

"Careful, woman, or I'll never get away from here!" he

growled with a good-natured chuckle. "I like your touch too much, Krystal."

She smiled. "I like everything about you, Gabe Marcos. Everything! What a spectacular way to make our own Christmas memories! I'll never forget . . ."

He kissed her again. "Me, either. How about a shower? I'll wash your—back."

"With an offer like that, how can I refuse?" She laughed and watched him roll from their bed—their Christmas, memory-making bed.

In the next few hours, when she was alone, Krystal manuevered to the sofa, enjoying the fire Gabe had left blazing merrily. She even managed to hop into the kitchen to make herself a cup of tea. The constant pain in her knee was gone. That was a good sign. Now it was a matter of letting it heal.

A Time of Staying Still.

Krystal gazed out the window at the silvery wonderland. She was surrounded by a beautiful Christmas-card landscape. What a wonderful way to spend Christmas! Miraculously she didn't feel the least bit lonely or regretful that she had been so confined. This was a Christmas she would always cherish. It seemed so absolutely right, so perfect, to be here with Gabe Marcos, in his strong arms.

A Time of Staying Still with Gabe.

He was a remarkable man: a leader who made people want to follow, a man of power, certainly; brazen, without being condescending; a good lover—no, an excellent one. She smiled, remembering. And yet he was sensitive. He cared, or seemed to, about her. He was just the kind of man she could fall in love with. And just the man she shouldn't! Oh dear God, she was losing her heart to him, and it scared her.

Deep inside Krystal knew she was treading on dangerous ground. She was definitely becoming emotionally involved with Gabe. She felt it happening, growing. And that was risky, considering . . .

She combed her hand through her hair the way he had done. Oh, dear, the sensations the man created in her! Just the thought of him sent her spinning. Perhaps she was infatuated with the lust he engendered whenever they were together.

She tossed her head as if to shake off her doubts. She would not worry about that now. Things were too magnificent between them to spoil with doubts. She wanted—needed—to relax and enjoy what was happening. She needed the Time of Staying Still with Gabe. It would be a marvelous Christmas to remember.

"Hey! Anybody here need a little physical therapy?"

Gabe's voice boomed into the room, and Krystal lifted her head sleepily. "Huh?"

"*Qué pasa?*"

Krystal found herself smiling even before she was fully awake. "Not very much. I fell asleep," she admitted sheepishly.

"Asleep, eh? Must have been a very good book." He entered the room loudly along with a blast of cold air.

She wrinkled her nose. "*Speed Skiing Made Easy.*"

He laughed and shrugged out of his ski jacket before sitting near her on the sofa. "Well, that's one bit of information you don't need, but maybe this is something you can use. *Felizes Navidades,* Krystal." He smiled widely, slipping a large box into her hands.

"A present? But Gabe, I don't have one for you. Oh, you shouldn't have . . ." Her emerald eyes grew large.

"I know. But I wanted to. Go ahead and open it."

Her hands tore excitedly at the silver wrapping until they rested on the softness within the box. "Oh, Gabe . . ." She lifted a varicolored poncho, hand woven of wool dyed brilliant shades of turquoise and red. "It's gorgeous!"

"You'll be pleased to know it's made right here in the Sangre de Cristos. Even the wool's from New Mexican sheep!" He helped her slide it over her head. "The colors are perfect for you, *mi amor.* It's called Navajo Rainbow Plaid."

"Oh, Gabe, you shouldn't have, but I'm glad you did! I love it!" She hugged him joyfully, pulling him near her pounding heart. "Thank you!"

He kissed her quickly. "How about that physical therapy now? We mustn't forget about your knee."

"The hot tub! Oh, yes!" she agreed enthusiastically.

"Well, this just won't do," he explained as he began unwrapping the Ace bandage from her knee. "You can't possibly have physical therapy with this thing on. Or this." His hands easily manipulated the buttons on her thigh-length shirt, caressing and teasing tender skin along the way.

"There, now! Perfect!" He eased the shirt from her shoulders and rocked back to admire her shivering nudity.

"If nude is perfect, then you've got it! But I'm cold!" She clutched the rainbow poncho to her breasts.

He kissed her nose quickly and quipped, "Oh, no you aren't! A hot-blooded vixen like you?" Then he swept Krystal, poncho and all, into his arms. They moved swiftly through the living room and into the bedroom. Past the bed, he pulled the wall-to-wall drapes aside and held her before the glass door. There, with the backdrop of the snow-covered Sangre de Cristo Mountains, was a redwood deck and the shimmering blue waters of a hot tub!

"Oh, Gabe, how beautiful!"

He pushed the door open and lowered her into the steamy ripples. As the warm, inviting water crept around her quivering form, it distorted the curved, feminine shapes now so familiar to him. It was all he could do to keep from plunging in, clothes and all.

"Ah, Gabe, this is heaven!" Krystal sighed and wriggled delightedly until she was submerged up to her neck. "Now this is my style! I love it!"

"Me, too." He was already shedding his sweater.

Her feminine curiosity piqued, Krystal leaned back with pleasure and a steady smile to watch him undress. The midday sun glistened on his bare shoulders, creating something of an aura around his nude male form. He unzipped his slacks and discarded them, along with his briefs. His hard brown body contrasted with the glittering white snow beyond the deck. What a spectacular sight! She delighted in the physical virility of him, seeing his shoulder and arm muscles long and lean, his waist trim and taut, his legs sinewy and strong from skiing, all of him sleek like a mountain lion. Then he was beside her, pulling her moist, resilient body to his.

It was wonderful, the hour they spent frolicking in the hot tub. He caressed her, delighting in teaching Krystal newfound pleasures of underwater sensations. Together they laughed as her breasts responded to his teasing touch, her nipples pouting immediately beneath his fingertips. The creamy mounds seemed to float right out of the water, eager for more teasing. He stroked and massaged her achy muscles. His capable hands manipulated her legs, helping her bend the injured one slightly, then creating a tingly underwater trail along her thighs.

Flushed with the warm stimulation, Krystal kissed him, penetrating his willing lips with her exploring tongue. Her hands slid curiously over his wet, slick muscles. She marveled at the feel of his forearms and chest, pausing to squeeze the tight male nipples that responded immediately to her touch. Raking her hands down his flat belly and around to his buttocks, Krystal delighted in stroking their slightly rounded shape. She smiled with satisfaction as his quivering manhood enhanced magnificently at her touch.

"Krystal, come here." Skillfully he pulled her over his aroused form.

"In here?" She laughed. "We'll have a little manuevering problem, won't we?"

"Not if I hold you tight. Like this." His hands grasped her buttocks, digging sensuously into the soft flesh. He forced her thighs against his, and she could feel his hardness rise to meet her feminine warmth.

By wrapping one leg around his hips, she was able to settle herself tightly over him. Together they rode to the summit, their bodies glistening in the New Mexico sunlight. Surrounded by the silvery snow-covered landscape of the magnificent mountains, they reached the heights of ecstasy, forgetting the risks of feelings and emotions and hearts.

When they finally floated apart, she smiled. "I never knew it could be so good, Gabe."

His hand spread on her shoulder. "Come on, *querida.* I think we've been in the water long enough. I don't want you to shrivel up to a prune!" He scooped her up in his arms and carried her, dripping, inside to the bed.

Gently he laid her there, wrapping her in the top blanket. Then he slid inside and curled her against him.

"What a refreshing hot tub you have," Krystal quipped, wiping water droplets from his chest.

He nuzzled the moist tendrils behind her ear. "What a nice, relaxing way to spend Christmas . . ."

Krystal smiled happily as she snuggled deeper in his arms.

Later that night they ate lamb stew and warm, buttered corn tortillas in front of the fireplace. Gabe opened an aged bottle of Blanco Malvasia Rioja he had saved from a trip to Spain. The fire crackled merrily, and the special aroma of mesquite wood permeated the air. Sounds of seasonal tunes, some sung in Spanish, filtered from the radio. The mood was relaxed and mellow.

"Gabe, this has been a wonderful Christmas."

His hand slid down her leg and rested light on her knee. "Even with the injury? And not being with your family?"

"Yep. I didn't miss them at all."

"Me, either." He shrugged as if it didn't matter, but Krystal knew better. "This is where I wanted to be, Krystal. I'm only sorry we missed the Pueblos' Deer Ceremony today. They always dance on Christmas Day, and when I'm here I try to go. I'll bet they were spectacular this year in the snow. Maybe next year."

"Do they let strangers in?" She took his hand and placed it against her cheek.

"I could get us an invitation."

Kissing the palm of his hand, she touched her tongue to the center. "Do you have friends in high places?"

He smiled. "Something like that." Then he bent to kiss the sweet skin on her neck.

Krystal shivered at the sensation. "I thought you always went to your sister's for Christmas."

He shifted and settled his head warmly in her lap. "Not always. Sometimes she brings her family here. But we usually try to spend it together."

"Sorry I kept you from doing that this year, Gabe." Her hand buried in his hair, mussing the silky blackness.

"I'd rather be with you."

"I'm glad." Krystal leaned over and kissed him. "What did you tell her?"

"That a beautiful blond green-eyed witch hexed me, and I was under her spell!" He hooked his hand behind her head and held her for another kiss.

"Oh, you!" She ruffled his hair.

"Anaya understands. They're coming up next week. They'd probably rather do that, anyway. I know I prefer it. The first few years after I opened the resort, I was too busy to leave, so Anaya and her family came here. It was great fun for them and gave me a chance to repay a small portion of all that she has done for me. I love sharing with her. At slack times in the season I go to Santa Fe and spend time with them." Talking about his family seemed to come easy for him.

"Sounds as though you have a good relationship with your sister." She stared into the blazing fireplace.

A warmth lit his eyes. "Very. She's four years older than I am and helped put me through school after Dad died. So a few years ago I returned the favor by sending her back to finish college. She had one child and was expecting another by the time she graduated. She looked like a blimp under that black cap and gown. God, we teased her!"

"But she finished, didn't she?" Krystal drew a line

down the middle of his face, touching him because she couldn't help herself.

"Oh, yes! I don't know who was more proud of her, me or her husband, Thom! Now, as a Spanish-speaking English teacher, she's very much in demand."

"You seem very proud of her."

"I am. She's terrific. I want you to meet her, Krystal."

"I'd like that." Krystal wanted to think it was significant that he considered introducing her to his family. She hoped it meant something special. But she didn't dare press. She was afraid of spoiling this new, precious relationship they had.

"Anaya's a lot like our mother, who was a remarkable woman. I was fourteen when my father—when he died. Mamá lost her home and her husband at the same time. It was unbelievably tough, but she pulled us through."

Krystal noticed that a pall had closed over his expression, and she encouraged him to continue. "What did you do?" She covered his hand with her own.

"We moved to Santa Fe, where my mother had relatives. Lived in the barrio. There isn't much for a minority woman to do, but we managed. We all worked hard. That's why I can't do enough for Anaya. I never got to—repay Mamá. She died the year before I bought the lodge."

"Oh, Gabe . . ." Krystal murmured helplessly. Her arm encircled his chest. For all the rumors, she now knew there was a vulnerability beneath that steel surface. And he had revealed it to her.

"*Por Dios,* I don't know why I told you all that, Krystal," he muttered, obviously embarrassed.

"I'm glad you did. It helps me know you better."

"Okay, it's confession time. Tell me more about Krystal

North, bewitching, green-eyed mystery woman!" He reached up and touched her hair. "What about you? Do you always go to Jason's for Christmas?"

She sighed, trying to switch her thoughts from the Marcos family to her own. "No. Last year was—awful." Her voice sounded strange, and Krystal realized that she hadn't talked about that experience very much. Maybe it was time to say it, to express aloud what a bad time it had been. Perhaps it was safe to tell someone who cared.

"Your sister was ill then?"

Krystal nodded. "Margo was in and out of the hospital during December. It's terrible to spend the holidays in a hospital. I can't even remember what we did on Christmas Day. Oh yes . . ." She grew thoughtful. "Jason and Meg brought dinner and a few gifts. It was very low-key and sad. We all knew it was Margo's last."

"When did she die?"

"In January."

"Krystal, you still feel a great deal of pain over her death, don't you?" His voice was sincere, and he was sitting now, clasping her hands securely.

She looked in his eyes and felt that he could probably read her thoughts, even her emotions. "It was so unfair! She was only twenty-six when she died!"

"Sometimes life isn't very fair."

"Oh, Gabe, it was hell. We knew she was dying. She knew it, too. She slipped away very fast." She turned her face away to hide the swell of emotions the memories brought.

"I'm sorry, Krystal. I know it hurts. I can see it. And I want to heal that pain. I wish I could." His voice was low and tender, with an amazing thread of understanding.

She turned away and wiped her tears silently. "Gabe—"

"There's more, isn't there, Krystal? Tell me . . . Sometimes it helps to talk about these things."

Later she wondered why she had said it. Perhaps she just needed to share the heavy burden. "Margo had been very ill and confided in me that she didn't want the misery of her life prolonged. I listened, not realizing what she was saying. I thought she meant the therapy."

Gabe was close beside her, his hands resting on her shoulders. He was strong and caring and, she was convinced, could help stop her pain. Her words were slow and sorrowful, dwindling to a low rasp. "She waited until—after Christmas. Until she could stand no more. Then—she took—all the pills."

His hands gripped her fiercely, and his head reeled. "*Por Dios,* Krystal! What are you saying?"

"That Margo's dying wasn't natural. She chose the time. I'm the only one, besides the doctor, who knows."

"Oh, my God, Krystal!" Gabe's arms encircled her, pressing her to the warmth, the security, of his chest. Her salty tears fell on his sweater, and he held her until she had cried herself dry.

Finally Krystal spoke haltingly. "I felt so guilty, so responsible. What could I have done to stop her? I should have read the signs. I'm sure there were some. It was so hard to understand, to bear. I didn't even tell Jason—couldn't. Somehow I was sure it was my fault."

"Oh, no, *querida.* It wasn't your fault. You can't bear the responsibility for the actions of others. Even someone as dear as your own sister."

"But we were so close. I was with her. I should have known. She even said—"

"I know, I know. But you aren't at fault. It's been a

year, and time to shed that guilt. Now is the time for healing and growing strong again."

She looked at him, huge tears shimmering in her emerald eyes. "I have not been strong through all this. I finally reached a point when I couldn't face that shop—our shop—again. There were just too many memories around. I jumped at the chance to move to High Valley."

"I can understand that."

"You are so good for me, Gabe. Thank you for listening. I'm glad I came up here—glad I spent Christmas with you."

"So am I."

"Hold me, Gabe . . ." she whispered.

With great tenderness he held her throughout the night. But Krystal couldn't see the veil of confusion and sorrow in Gabe's deep blue eyes as he stared into the blackness long after she slept in his arms. Now what would he do? Her commitment to High Valley was as strong as his, maybe stronger. She needed it, needed him. And he was drawn to her, more than he had ever believed possible. This was certainly not what he had planned. He had never intended to care so deeply for Krystal North.

His dark hand stroked her golden hair, relishing its silky texture, until it became entangled—just as he had unintentionally become entangled in her life, in caring for her.

CHAPTER EIGHT

She sighed, looking out at the gray sky, and answered wistfully, "Yes, Jason. I had a very nice Christmas. And you?"

"A little hectic, but with two four-year-olds, what can you expect? Missed you, Krystal."

"I missed you, too. When can you bring Meg and the twins up to the mountains?"

"Not for a few weeks yet. I'm swamped with a couple of major projects right now."

"Maybe by the time you come, I'll have one of the cottages livable for you. If it's not a fallen roof, it's an overflowing toilet. Right now Vegas is working on chipped plaster, before the walls cave in along with the roof!"

"Do you need help up there, Krystal?"

"I'm going to become an *enjarradora* and plaster the walls myself. I'd probably make more money!" She laughed a little, but both of them knew the serious implications of her statement.

"Krystal, don't you want to bail out now, before you sink any more money into this dinosaur? Eking out a living on that mountain can't be what you're after."

"I'm not on the mountain. I happen to be located in the golden valley between two mountains. It's prime property, Jason! And no, I don't have any intentions of bailing out."

"Krystal—"

"And I don't want to discuss if further."

"Okay. Can we talk about your health? How's the injured leg?"

"Oh, fine. I'm buzzing around almost as good as new. Of course, no more skiing!"

"Actually, hon, you should have your head examined for going in the first place after that accident you had a few years back. How are things with you and Marcos? You sounded as though you two were pretty chummy for a while."

Chummy? Krystal bristled, but she tried to keep her voice calm. Should she tell Jason that she hadn't heard from the man since she left the warm folds of his cabin?

"Oh, yes, we're still friends . . ." It was such a little lie, she hoped Jason would forgive her. Anyway, she assumed they were some sort of friends, after all they had shared.

"Has your *friend* agreed to the merger yet?"

"I'm still working on it, Jason."

"Well, better speed up the process, hon. The state tax people are screaming down my neck. And need I remind you that the time for paying the inheritance tax to the IRS is right around the corner?"

"No, you needn't remind me, Jason," she answered stiffly. "I'll get to work on it."

"Krystal, are you all right?"

"Sure." She forced a small chuckle.

"I, uh, know January is a bad month for you, with memories of Margo. Why don't you come down and stay with us for a few weeks?" His voice was gentle.

"I appreciate the invitation, Jason, but I can't. I need to keep busy these days, and this place surely provides plenty of work to keep me occupied. Anyway, how can I encourage the merger if I'm not up here?" She hoped she sounded convincing. Actually she didn't want to risk missing Gabe. What if he called today? Immediately she realized that she was planning her life around a possibility—and a remote one at that.

"I hate to say it, but you're going to lose it unless you can make it profitable. And pretty soon."

"Thanks for your optimism. I'll be in touch," she said.

"Krystal, I care what happens. Honest to God! I want to help you if you'll let me."

"I know, Jason. Thanks." She tempered her tone, knowing she was edgy. It wasn't just the property taxes and the year's anniversary of Margo's death. Now Gabe Marcos's image haunted her day and night.

She cradled the phone and gazed longingly out her office window. There had been no snow and not much sunshine since Christmas; just gray, cloudy days. And no Gabe. She had stayed with him until two days after Christmas. He had helped her home and had been away "on business" since. She knew his sister and her family were coming up. Perhaps the excuse of business was a ruse he used to ensure his privacy with them. But why didn't he just tell her that? She would understand. He hadn't even called. *Why?* He had suggested that he wanted Anaya to meet her. Apparently he had changed his mind.

Changed his mind about a lot of things . . .

Once again Krystal doubted herself. Had she been a first-class fool to go to bed with him? To stay with him? To fall in love with him? Love? Oh, no . . . not really. It's too soon for that. Infatuation, maybe. Intrigue, certainly. But love?

Krystal sighed, knowing that love with the fabled Gabe Marcos was far too risky for someone in her shoes. She needed security, wanted a commitment. And he certainly wasn't the commitment type. She knew that much about him.

So where did that leave her? On the outside, looking in! It was frightening, knowing she had made a huge mistake, knowing that all she had left in the world—High Valley Ranch—might soon be taken away from her. And Gabe Marcos as well.

No, she decided determinedly. Not if I have anything to say about this. Not if I have an ounce of strength to fight it! She tapped her pencil calculatingly against the desk top. She wouldn't give up so easily on the land—or on Gabe Marcos.

"Krystal, why do I have the feeling I'm being seduced?" Candlelight flickered angular shadows across his dark features, but nothing could dim those blue Spanish eyes.

Just the sight of Gabe sent Krystal's heart pounding wildly. Oh, God, he still had that same enchanting ability to send her spinning as he had the first night they met. That spell-weaving enchantment was stirring tonight. She could feel it.

"Why, Gabe, I just wanted to repay your—gracious hospitality. Didn't you enjoy it?" She tried to keep her voice light and steady.

He motioned to their empty plates. "It was superb. The scampi was magnificent. I haven't had shrimp cooked that way since a trip I made last year to San Francisco. Yours was excellent!"

She smiled charmingly with the knowledge that the menu, at least, had been a good choice. It had been quite an effort to go all the way to Santa Fe for the shrimp. And it was damn expensive, too! Money well spent, she calculated.

"I'm glad you liked it, Gabe." It was an offhand remark. She was very pleased with the way the evening was proceeding. Krystal was exceedingly cool, which was just the way she had intended being. Gabe was—curious, but tolerant. Things were still going according to plan.

Gabe's warm hand covered hers. "You knew I would enjoy anything you cooked." Then he moved his hand, as if the continued touch burned him. He shifted uneasily.

"Actually, I didn't know for sure that you liked shrimp. In fact, there's so much I don't know about you, Gabe."

He chuckled tersely. "You know more than most, Krystal."

"But I want to know everything." Her hand slid over his, and she could feel a tiny muscle spasm from his hand against her palm.

Gabe shifted in his chair, removing his hand in the process. "I don't think that's possible. I'm usually a very private person. To be quite honest, I don't normally take women into my cabin. I've never lived with a woman."

"Then why did you bother with me? I asked to leave." Krystal narrowed her emerald eyes, and candlelight reflected some of the exasperation she felt. Once he took her in his arms, she was willing to stay with him forever.

He heaved a sigh. "I don't know. I'm still questioning myself about that."

"Is that where you were for the last two weeks? Questioning yourself?" She rose and walked over to the coffee pot, pouring them each a cup with shaky hands.

"Yes, as a matter of fact, that's exactly what I did over the last two weeks!" He sounded almost angry. Upset, surely.

She kept her back to him. "Any answers?"

"I've come to the conclusion that I have no regrets about what has happened between us. Have you?"

She turned around, gripping the steaming cup tightly. "No regrets, Gabe. Some questions, though. A woman doesn't easily shrug off a relationship with a man who introduces her to so much—happiness."

"I know. I haven't been fair to you, Krystal. But I don't have any more answers. Not yet, anyway."

She handed him the hot cup of coffee. "Shall we go into the living room where it's more comfortable?"

In silence they entered the small, comfortable room, each avoiding the sofa. That would force them to sit too close together. Right now, anyway. They chose separate chairs and faced each other.

Gabe broke the uncomfortable silence. His voice was low toned and velvet. "You deserve some answers, Krystal, but I'm not sure I can give them to you."

"I just want to know how you feel. About us." Krystal smiled faintly, half afraid of what he might say, but needing to know.

He gestured futilely with one hand. "I can't tell you that, either. After Christmas I returned to Santa Fe with Anaya and Thom. I needed the time away."

"Away from me?"

He looked up quickly, an intent expression on his face. "Yes, if you must know. From you, Krystal. You see, you are like the constant desert wind. I can't get you off my mind."

"And you want to." It was a cold statement, and she feared his response.

"Yes—no! My God, no! I want to hold you and love you every minute! Every day! Every night!"

A slow, enticing smile spread across her face. This was

the answer she'd hoped for, prayed for. "Good. I'm glad the misery is mutual, Gabe. It's that magic you spoke of when we first met. Do you remember? Only now it's more powerful than ever."

He drank his coffee and set the cup on the low table between them with an impatient rattle. "Oh, yes. I remember well. The only trouble is, I don't believe in magic."

"Then it was a line, just as I thought it was?" She was smiling, but inside she felt a tight, painful knot growing, threatening to choke her.

He grinned a devilish grin, smiling for the first time that night. "You're smart enought to see through me or any other man who's trying to manipulate you."

"Maybe I wanted to be manipulated—that night. By you."

"Did you?"

"I was vulnerable then. Not now." She was lying through her teeth and hoped he couldn't see it. She was much more vulnerable now, because her heart was involved.

"What about now? Tonight?" His eyes asked the deeper, more intimate question.

"I invited you here for several reasons, Gabe. I want to know how you feel—about us. I don't want to lose what we've had. It has been wonderful and could be again. I want to be loved again by you. But I don't want to be used."

He stood and began to pace nervously. "I . . . I don't know if I can promise anything, Krystal. I don't know if I'm capable."

"Or if you want to be capable."

A heavy silence preceded his response. "Maybe you're right. I want to be free. You have intruded in my life and are weighing heavily on my mind, wreaking havoc with my plans—not to mention a complete night's sleep!"

She set her cup down deliberately. "Sorry I've been such an inconvenience to you, Gabe. You know, you haven't exactly been a blessing in my life, either. My days are filled with thinking of you—wondering what will happen to us. My nights are just as sleepless and lonely."

He shook his head woefully. "Krystal, I'm sorry, I don't know what to tell you."

"Fortunately, there are some solutions. If I could prove the magic, would you believe it?" she asked.

"Can you?" He arched a dark brow, and an expression of amusement lit his eyes.

She met his gaze steadily, raising her chin defiantly. "Can you look at me without remembering our Christmas together? How you took care of me when I was injured—the laughter and secrets we shared—the fun in the hot tub—the ways we made love."

His voice was low and gentle. "You know that time was special for both of us. Of course I remember every detail of being with you!" In the next moment he was on one knee, next to her legs, his arms embracing her thighs. "Krystal, kiss me. Just touch me . . ."

She leaned forward, and their lips met with such ferocity that she gripped his shoulders tightly and moaned with the painful pressure. His lips forced hers open, his teeth nipping sharply as his tongue plundered fiercely. She barely had time to think, to react. Then he sought the pulse at the base of her throat, kissing and nibbling with hard teeth against her tender skin.

"Does that answer your question? I want you, *querida,*" he said, his voice muffled against her burning skin.

"I want you, too, Gabe," she gasped, breathless and

shaken. She inched slender fingers along his neck, digging into the ebony hair that pressed against her breast. He had responded the way she had hoped, planned. She was the seductress tonight. She was in control.

As abruptly as he had come to her, he moved away. "No! It isn't fair to you, Krystal. I can't give you what you need. I can make no promises!" He paced and ran a shaking hand around the back of his neck. "I just can't. I swore to myself I wouldn't hurt you. I'm afraid I already have."

Krystal stood, gathering her strength from the energy of their kiss, from his sheer masculine presence, from her love for him. She couldn't let him go now. They were too close. She wanted him desperately. And in her heart, she was convinced he wanted her, too.

"Gabe," she said quietly. "I want you to stay with me tonight."

He didn't look at her, and his answer was quick and cold. Perhaps he had practiced it. "I can't. I have to get back to the lodge. Early tomorrow morning we're spraying artificial snow."

She stood beside him, feeling his energy, hearing his labored breathing. Taking his hand, she pressed it to her own pounding heart. "You can go back early tomorrow. I want you tonight. I can make no promises, either."

His hand tensed, and she heard his sharp intake of air as she slid his palm to her soft, inviting breast.

"Krystal . . ." he said with a groan.

"I'm serious, Gabe. I want you to make love to me tonight. I know the risks. And I'm willing to gamble. One more night—please."

He turned his face to her, astonished at her boldness, rent apart by her plea. With his other hand he stroked her face, then buried his fingers in the warmth at the base of her neck. "*Mi querida . . .*" He pulled her to him, molding her feminine curves to his masculine hardness.

Regardless of what he said, his body betrayed him. Krystal knew he had reacted to her first touch. His heart pounded against hers, and she could feel his heat, his energy. Now, as they stood in an embrace, his rigid masculinity rose boldly between them, assuring her of his real desire for her. She could only hope for love.

"Should I carry you into my bedroom?" She chuckled softly.

He bent to nuzzle her neck. "Hmmm, I'm so weak with desire, you may have to. God, I want you."

Her hands slid under his sweater to caress the ridges of muscle along his backbone. "I'm not sure if I can carry you, Gabe. You're a little above my weight class. Maybe I could drag you!" They laughed, and some of the old, wonderful humor they had shared returned. He bent to kiss her, his lips branding her with desire.

"Take me, Gabe . . ."

Trancelike, they moved into her bedroom, each stripping off the clothes that encumbered their lovemaking. He stood waiting, eager, patient, torn with emotion at the sight of her standing bare and shimmering before him. Flickering lights from the candles in the other room danced over her creamy breasts and silken thighs. She looked like an apparition as she took a step toward him.

Gabe sucked in his breath sharply, forcing himself to unhurried leisure. Otherwise he would take her immediately and spoil everything between them. Oh God, he did not want to ruin what they had. It was too special. It was indeed magic, even though he tried to deny it.

"Touch me, Gabe," she whispered temptingly.

He obliged, slowly at first, savoring every warm,

smooth curve of her body. Almost tentatively his long fingers graced her shoulders and arms, sending shivers of eager anticipation through her. His large hands encircled her waist and traveled the straight lines of her back before cupping each rounded hip. Instinctively he pulled her to him for a moment, pressing her loins to his. Krystal felt herself go limp against his hardness.

He lingered on her breasts, lightly plucking the soft tips until they grew to knots of ripened fullness. Pressing his palms to their softness, he kneaded them gently while he kissed her, then bent to kiss each aching mound. His hands ran over her length, caressing the feminine shapes, stroking the quivering quicksilver at the core of her femininity.

Krystal purred softly, and it was with great effort that she pushed herself away. "Now it's my turn," she whispered huskily.

Her soul sang with lyrics of sweet love as her hands played the sinewy strings of his finely tuned body. He shivered with desire as her slender fingers stroked each muscle, searching for its beginning, continuing down its length, rejoicing in the harmonious combination of strength and softness.

She reached around to rake her nails lightly over the muscles in his back, while her aroused nipples tickled his chest. He groaned, but before he could raise his arms to encompass her, she gripped them and sketched their definition with teasing fingers.

"Krystal . . ."

"Not yet," she said huskily.

Her devilish hands continued their eager music, memorizing his virile shape, beguiling his endurance, enhancing his magnificent masculine splendor.

In another moment he pulled her against him, molding her simmering form to his flaming passion. "That's it!" he managed raggedly. "I can't wait any longer for you!"

His knee pushed her legs apart, and by the time they were on the bed, he was possessing her, plundering her deep sweetness. Their passion was unified in one wild, glorious symphony of ecstasy as their rhythm synchronized to a spellbinding beat. The magic was in motion, something neither could deny or avoid. It was unbelievable yet real, bewitching yet wonderful. The enchantment encompassed them, merged them in an act of love and a compulsive, vigorous climax that left each breathless and weak.

It was many glorious moments before either of them spoke. The spell of love was too awesome to break, and neither had the strength or desire to penetrate it.

"Oh, *querida,* I can't resist your love . . ." he murmured against her neck. "You see what you do to me, don't you? I'm weak in your arms."

Krystal's heart caught in her throat. Love? Was he talking about love? She kissed the dampness on his chest and wrapped her arms possessively around his ribs, pressing him into her even more. "That's the magic. I don't want you to resist it, Gabe, because I can't. My love is here for you—only you."

With a low, contented groan he gathered her in his arms and settled her against his chest. She could hear his heart pounding and smell his masculine fragrance. Pine and herbs and all outdoors—he reminded her of the mountain that he loved.

But what about his feelings? Did he love her as she did him? Was it something they could continue to deny?

"When I hold you like this, *querida,* I want to stay here in your arms forever."

"And when you're away?"

He sighed heavily. "I know it's not possible."

"Anything is possible if you want it badly enough."

"Is that your philosophy?"

"Gabe, right now I'm not sure what my philosophy is. Life has been very confusing for me. I suppose I like to dream that things will turn out well if all parties work toward that end."

"Don't dream too much, Krystal. Sometimes other things get in the way."

"Things? I think we're talking about different subjects, Gabe. I'm talking about people and feelings—about us."

"I just want you to be realistic. Sometimes a change of plans can be better than what was originally intended."

"What the hell are you talking about?"

He sighed. "This place, Krystal. It's falling apart. It's foolish to think you can renovate it into a viable business. It'll take too long and cost too much money."

"Not if you help me."

His hand stroked her arm, and ominous shivers washed over her. "Krystal, I would do anything to help you. *Anything!* I would loan you the money if I thought the investment were sound."

"I don't want you to loan me money. I want the merger so I can get the money on my own and repay you in profits."

"God, you're stubborn! Don't you see what I'm trying to say?"

If she did understand, she chose to ignore it. "No, I'm just determined to do this on my own."

His voice gentled, and he tried another tactic. "Krystal,

before you do anything else around here, I'd like to take you to Santa Fe. I want you to meet Anaya, anyway. We could look around."

Krystal smiled and scooted her hand up his chest to rest in a warm spot on his neck. "I'd like to meet her. Are you sure you're ready to introduce me to your family?" There was a taint of sarcasm in her voice. They had talked about this before, and he had avoided it when the time came.

"I—I'm ready this time. I told her about you. She wants to know this blond vixen who has me in such turmoil."

"I thought I was the one in turmoil." Krystal smiled, confident at least that he had some of the same feelings she did. Tonight they were as one, she was sure.

"I did some looking around for you while I was in Santa Fe."

"Looking around? There you go again. What are you talking about, Gabe?"

He paused and took a deep breath. "What if I helped you get set up in Santa Fe? It's an excellent city for a business such as yours. I agree that you shouldn't go back to Albuquerque. The memories of Margo are too painful there. But Santa Fe—"

"Wait!" She stiffened in his arms. "You want me to leave here?"

"I don't think this will work, Krystal. I'll help you find the perfect location for a new boutique there."

"You want me that far away from you?" The ranch was forgotten for an instant, and all she could think of was being away from Gabe, of losing him.

"I'll come to see you often in Santa Fe. It could be a place for us to meet."

"Then I would be your mistress?" The words soured in her mouth.

"Well, it wouldn't be—"

"No commitments, huh?" She spat the words out bitterly.

"Krystal, you need—"

"Don't tell me what I need," she interrupted with venom. "I know exactly what I need and what I don't need! You're right, I came here to High Valley Ranch to escape. I had to get away from the memories of my sister—from the guilt and sadness. I thought this place was perfect for me. My mistake was in thinking you were good for me, too, Gabe Marcos! I was a fool to think you would help solve my financial problems. Or that you would understand—really understand—my feelings."

"I understand more than you know, Krystal," he admitted in a low tone.

"Then why won't you consider the merger? I'll tell you! There's only one type of merger you want! And I've been all too willing for that!" She moved away from the warmth of his arms, angry with him, furious with herself. His motives were clear to her now.

Her words pierced him painfully. He understood and yet had been unwilling to give what she needed—what he alone could give her. Love!

"Krystal—" His hand cupped her chin.

"Don't touch me! You want this land and me, too. Now you think you've figured out a way to have both! Purchase the run-down ranch, take it off my hands and tuck me away for an occasional visit!"

"Listen to reason! That's not at all what I meant, *querida,*" he objected.

"No! I won't be your mistress! I've given too much of myself already! And I won't give up this land! Ever!" She hoped she sounded as though she had the money to back up her words.

Gabe flipped angrily onto his back, his arms folded under his head, and stared blindly at the black ceiling.

Krystal turned away from him. Bitter tears of frustration and intense pain streamed from her sad, dark emerald eyes.

Gabe returned to the lodge in a foul mood. Everywhere he looked, her blond hair enchanted him, her sensuous smile captivated him, her emerald eyes, now filled with tears, mesmerized him. Krystal . . . Krystal . . . what are you doing to me? Worse yet, what am I doing to you?

He was furious that a woman had this kind of power over him, could capture him like a snared animal. And he couldn't escape her face, her lingering fragrance, her image in every distance he viewed. There was no escape!

CHAPTER NINE

The final weeks of January seemed agonizingly long. Krystal thought the month would never end. She forced herself to go to Albuquerque to spend a few days with Jason and Meg. She couldn't bear being alone with only the sad memories of Margo's death to haunt her. And alone she was, for Gabe Marcos was not part of her life anymore. She had neither heard from nor seen him since that night . . . that fateful night when they had made love, then parted hurt and angry.

She welcomed the noisy chaos Jason's twin boys created and happily baby-sat several evenings. One night, when Meg and Jason returned, the three of them sat around the kitchen table with cups of cinnamon-flavored Mexican hot chocolate.

"We can't thank you enough for giving us this evening alone, Krystal." Meg beamed, slipping her hand affectionately through Jason's arm. "Tonight was so special. It's seldom that we can go out with no worries about the sitter or the kids—or both!"

"The pleasure was all mine, Meg. The kids are darling, and I love being with them. They're growing so fast, I can't believe it. Anyway, it's the very least I can do for you two. You've been so supportive, especially this last year." Krystal smiled warmly at Jason's wife. She was lucky to have them both. They were friends, family and business advisers.

Meg patted her hand. "We're family. We stick together in times like these. I know this year has been difficult for you, Krystal. It's hard to believe that Margo's been gone a year. We've all experienced a tremendous loss." There was a moment of uncomfortable silence at the reference to Margo's death.

"Yes, it's been a long, difficult year." Krystal sighed, then changed the subject quickly. "Well, how was the performance tonight?"

"Krystal, that was the best idea you've had in a long time," Jason answered enthusiastically. "You were right! The dance was magnificent! I have never seen flamenco performed with more precision and flair! The girl was terrific!"

Meg countered quickly, "I preferred the handsome guitarist. All his music was fantastic, but when he played 'Malagueña,' chills ran down my spine! Did you say you saw them in Taos?"

"Yes." Krystal nodded, remembering her "first date" with Gabe. "They're originally from Málaga, down in Andalusia, the part of Spain where flamenco is so dominant."

"How do you know so much about this couple?" Meg asked.

Krystal smiled. "They're protégés of our friend Gabriel Marcos."

"Ahha! The plot thickens!" Meg teased. "Sounds to me like there's more to this than meets the eye! Come on, Krystal, you can tell us what's going on between you two."

"Absolutely nothing!" Krystal declared, sadly truthful. "Just because I happen to know he brought two dancers to this country from Spain doesn't mean there's anything going on between us."

"And spent Christmas with him!" Meg pointed out.

"Yes." Krystal nodded. "But I'm still scrambling to get this business off the ground, aren't I?"

"Yep," Jason agreed. "Mr. Marcos has been less than cooperative in this endeavor."

"Oh, Krystal, I wish you weren't going back tomorrow. It's been such fun to have you here, but it just wasn't long enough. We didn't even have a chance to go shopping in Old Town Albuquerque." Meg sighed wistfully.

"I know, Meg, but I must get back to High Valley. I need to see what's fallen down this time! I don't know how my uncle ever lived in the place. Or maybe it just waited till this year to collapse!"

"Krystal, how are things going with Marcos?" Jason drove the subject back to business.

Shaking her head, Krystal admitted, "I hate to say this, Jason, but communications between Gabe Marcos and myself have broken down."

"I thought you had been awfully quiet about the situation between you two," Jason commented dryly.

"I don't think he'll ever consider a merger, Jason. I'll have to come up with the money some other way."

Jason rubbed his chin thoughtfully. "Has he finally refused?"

"No. But he has never discussed it seriously. He still insists on purchasing. I know he needs a new road. I've seen what a mess the old one is in bad weather. When it snows, he has a plow that does nothing but clear the road and lead the bus from the main highway to his resort. And there's always the risk of accidents when it ices."

"Sounds like the guy should jump at the chance for a

new access to his resort. Not to mention the year-round financial prospects your business could offer."

"The only thing he'd jump at would be the chance to buy the whole valley." And to have me in bed, she thought bitterly.

"I don't understand the man's single-mindedness," Jason protested. "For years now he's tried to buy that land, without success. Yet he refuses to give up or to give in an inch."

Krystal smiled wryly. "Gabe Marcos give up? No way! He's single-minded and stubborn. I don't really understand, but he mentioned that all the land surrounding High Valley and Starfire was once part of his family's vast sheep ranch. It belonged to them for several generations, but his father had to sell it. Now Gabe wants to get it all back."

"His family were sheepherders? Basques from Spain?" Meg asked.

Krystal nodded offhandedly. "Some generations back they migrated from Spain and developed a huge spread in New Mexico. But when his father died, his family lost the property."

Meg smiled. "You know, those old-generation Basque sheepherders were a special breed. Apparently they still are. Their attachment to the land was extremely strong, definitely an emotional involvement. They lived there, worked there and loved it intensely. They poured their hearts and souls into the land."

"Sounds like Gabe Marcos all right," Krystal murmured.

"How do you know all that?" Jason looked askance at his wife.

"I had a history teacher once whose family were

Basques. She delighted in relating tales of life on the sheep ranches. Even though they're Americans, they retain many of the old Spanish traditions even today." Meg mused quietly, "They say a man who sells his land sells his mother."

Krystal jerked her head up, a million thoughts racing through her mind. "What?"

"Oh, it's just an old expression that shows their deep dedication to the land. It's hard for others to understand that Mother Earth concept."

"Strange . . ." Jason pondered.

"No, it isn't. It all makes more sense now. The pieces are beginning to fit together. His strong family ties, some of the things he's said . . ." Krystal assessed slowly. She raised her emerald eyes. "I'll never get his help, Jason. He will never give in to what I'm asking."

Krystal's cousin tapped anxious fingers on the table. He could see by the stricken expression on her face that things were falling apart for her. "Maybe all is not lost, Krystal. Let me talk to Marcos's lawyer once more. It just doesn't make sense that a man would cling to such antiquated notions. After all, I notice he didn't go back to sheepherding on the mountain. He's running a very profitable, contemporary business. I'm sure some old-timers weren't happy to see him open up something that would attract thousands of tourists and plow out strips of virgin forest to make ski trails and roads."

"Oh, Gabe is very aware of what makes money. But he does it his way. Now he's planning a mountaintop restaurant that will be cantilevered over the edge of a cliff. It will have magnificent views of the mountains and . . ." Krystal's voice trailed as flashbacks of their picnic in the snow grew vivid. The wine . . . the strawberries . . . the kisses . . . oh, why couldn't she forget all that?

"Krystal?" Jason's voice penetrated her fog.

She lifted clear eyes. "I'm not holding out hope any longer that Gabe will ever come around to my way of thinking, Jason."

"We can try again. It won't hurt, surely. I'll admit he does sound like a stubborn SOB."

"Well, maybe he's met his match. I have no intention of selling out. That valley is mine now, and I want to stay there. Can you look into the chances of other financing, Jason?"

He pressed his lips together, pondering the possibilities that were available to Krystal. "I'll see what I can do, hon. Won't be easy. We may have to lower our expectations and borrow less money in the beginning."

She smiled grimly. "Well, that's nothing new, Jason. I can be stubborn, too."

Jason laughed and patted her shoulder approvingly. "Yes, Krystal, you certainly can be!"

Although Krystal sounded tough and defiant, she knew that she was still vulnerable to Gabe Marcos's magic. She just hoped she could defy his stubborn strength and make it her own way, without him. She returned to High Valley Ranch with that determination strong.

A breath-tightening web of apprehension enclosed Krystal's chest the minute she heard the Bronco roar into the High Valley Ranch complex. Oh, dear God, she prayed quickly. Give me strength to face Gabe Marcos.

"Krystal?" He called her name even before his heavy boots hit the brick porch.

She waited quietly, trying to calm herself as he walked

into High Valley Ranch's main room. His footsteps echoed against the empty walls. Then came the anticipated knock on her office door. Her heart pounded almost as loudly. Just as she expected, he opened the door without waiting for an answer.

Gabe stood in the doorway, his feet apart, his hands on narrow hips, looking so damn masculine and appealing. A knot formed quickly in Krystal's middle as her feelings for this man surfaced. Determinedly she fought their exposure. Damn him! I won't let him know! I'm stubborn, too.

She gazed silently, outwardly calm.

"Where have you been?" he demanded, as if she should report to him.

Resisting the urge to tell him it was none of his damn business, Krystal answered quietly, "I've been in Albuquerque with my family."

"Krystal, I—I know this month has been hard for you. I tried to reach you. I didn't intend for you to be alone." There was something unusual in his tone.

"I wasn't, thank you." She struggled to remain cool, all the while wanting to scream at him and perhaps fling the nearest item she could get her hands on. But, of course, she didn't. She smiled tightly.

"Krystal, I'm sorry."

"About what?" Damn you! About playing with my emotions until I fell headlong in love with you?

"About your sister and what you've gone through since her death. I know it's been hell. And I guess you deserve to escape and start over. I—I haven't been very understanding and supportive."

"What gave you sudden insight into my view?" She couldn't hide the bitterness she felt.

"I have always known—felt—you were hurting. From the first."

"Is that why you thought you could manuever me? Because you knew that I was vulnerable?"

"No, Krystal. I didn't try to take advantage of you. You have to believe me! There is—was something special between us."

Was? With a dry mouth, her voice rasped, "Yes. I think it's called lust!"

"Krystal, please don't degrade what we shared."

"Is that all you came over to say, Gabe? I have a lot of work to do." She hoped her tone would dismiss him. Now was not the time to discuss their relationship. Anyway, he had indicated that it was over, and though she ached inside at the knowledge, she would not let him see her pain.

"No. I came to take you somewhere. I have something to show you."

"I'm too busy, Gabe." She shook her head.

He strode to the desk, looming before her. "I want you to come with me. It won't take very long—a few hours, maybe. Please. It's very important. It will help you understand me."

"What if I don't care?" It was a venomous remark.

"I think you do."

She looked down and took a calming breath. "All right, I do care, Gabe. Perhaps too much for my own good. But that's something I can't help. When I go to bed with a man, my emotions are involved. I can't turn them off as easily as some people can. Believe me, though, I'm trying."

Gabe's hand closed over hers as he leaned on the desk. "Neither can I."

What was he saying? She felt like a jellyfish inside and thought for a wild moment that she would melt in his arms. Fighting the urge, her comments were tinged with ire. "Oh, sure! I should have paid heed to those rumors I heard before I met you. As a victim of Gabe Marcos's magic, I'm living proof of being the perfect fool. Just another of Gabe Marcos's fools!"

"Don't say that!" He was around the desk, grabbing both her forearms and pulling her fiercely against his chest. "You know that's not true. What happened between us was real. The feelings are still there! Can't you see that?"

"Real? The whole thing was one damn illusion! Let me go!"

"Damnit, Krystal, what I'm feeling right now isn't sympathy." He pushed her from him, his blue eyes fierce and sharp. He ran his hand around the back of his neck, then turned to her and repeated, "Come with me. I want to show you something I've never shown anyone else. Then maybe you'll understand why my desire for this land is so strong."

Krystal looked at him quizzically. What was he talking about? Later she wondered if it was curiosity or something greater that had made her agree to go. Deep inside she knew it was because she still couldn't resist him.

She allowed him to help her into the rainbow-colored poncho. She forced herself to hold her memories of the gift and those wonderful, love-filled days and nights in the cabin below the surface. They sat stubbornly quiet while the Bronco made its way behind the adobe buildings of High Valley Ranch. Rolling past the boulders and tree-surrounded natural hot springs, they found a faint path of a road that Krystal hadn't known existed.

Further and further into the depths of her property they rode, while Krystal gazed curiously out the window at aspects of the land she had never seen. She and Jason had rented a Cessna and flown over it once, but this part had appeared so uninhabitable that she hadn't paid much attention. Now, up close, it looked different—friendlier and more livable. The growth was sparse, but Krystal could picture sheep grazing on the hillsides.

"I haven't been up this road in twenty-one years." Gabe's voice broke into the stillness.

"Was this where you watched sheep when you were young?" Krystal looked at the rolling, semibarren hills, trying to imagine a boy with black hair and blue eyes herding flocks of black-faced, woolly-white sheep.

His nod was barely discernible. "This was where we lived."

She raised curious eyebrows. "Oh." She saw the area as it really was, stark and somewhat harsh. He viewed it with different eyes, she could tell. However, there was no comparing this bare landscape with the beauty of the mountain where Gabe now lived. So what drew him here?

Gabe fell again into brooding silence as they jostled over eroded tracks in the rugged terrain. Finally they pulled to a stop before a seemingly empty hillside.

Gabe took a deep breath and let it out raggedly. Without a word he opened the door and hauled his body out of the Bronco as if he were in slow-motion. He stumbled alone over the rocky soil, his face set in a somber expression. His jaws clenched tightly together, and his blue eyes darted across the New Mexico landscape, searching, absorbing.

Krystal waited for a few minutes, and when he didn't return, she stepped out, too. A strong, constant wind whipped around them, its flow unhalted by the scrubby trees. Krystal's blond hair flew wildly, like an unruly aura around her head. Her hand pinned it to her neck as she approached him.

"Why did we stop here, Gabe?"

He cast her a stony stare. "This is it, Krystal. This is my old homestead, where I grew up."

She glanced around, puzzled. "Where? Where is the house?"

Abruptly his flinty eyes softened, and he chuckled at her naiveté. Aiming a finger toward an earthy embankment, he said, "There. We lived in a genuine earth home. Nowadays they call them earth shelters."

"Oh?" Krystal couldn't picture living here in this remote place. She had assumed earth homes were a modern contrivance. Impulsively she took his hand. In doing so she created a physical bond between them again, a wonderful, touching bond that had existed once but had been severed by the individual, selfish drives of two stubborn, single-minded people.

"Come on and show me, Gabe. I want to see it up close."

For a second she thought she saw a flicker of warmth in his hard blue eyes before he led her toward an embankment. They braced themselves against the strong wind. It was just the two of them, alone in a solitary world.

"The years have taken their toll. It's in pretty bad condition," he remarked half to himself when they had approached the run-down shelter. "There's the door. And vines have grown over the windows—the only two windows in the entire place."

Krystal stared at the structure. It was an awesome experience, like stepping back in time, as they viewed the tawny house made of brown earth. Although it was not beautiful in the conventional sense, there was a primitive attraction here in this place, this home that was still part of the earth. Meg's words returned to prey on her mind. "They poured their hearts and souls into the land."

"I can't imagine living here, Gabe," Krystal confessed honestly.

Gabe pulled his hand from hers and tugged at some scraggly weeds that were growing in the earthen edifice. Then he said something that shook her to the core.

"I hated it. The little room where I slept was dark, with no windows. I can still remember the terrible, close feeling." He chuckled self-consciously. "I guess that's one reason I love a house that has lots of glass. A sweeping view of my surroundings is important to me. I need space and the feeling of freedom it gives me."

Krystal nodded. "I can understand that. A room with no windows must have been scary for a little boy." She tried to imagine what Gabe had been like as a child. Stubborn and hard? Gullible and loving? Shy? Arrogant? Affectionate? He was all those things now.

Gabe kicked a loose stone boyishly and ambled over to sit on a gnarled, dead cedar. He talked as if he were in a trance, and Krystal moved near so she could hear him.

"We played out here. Anaya and I chased each other across the roof and jumped off over there by the front door. We had a pen for the sheep down there, and an old weathered barn for the equipment. Now the barn is completely gone. Everything else was sold at auction the day my father—died. He just couldn't stand the thought of losing all this land that had been handed down through generations of Marcoses. Everything he had worked for all his life was gone."

Krystal was drawn closer to him. Maybe it was his tone. Maybe . . . something intangible. "Oh, Gabe, how awful to lose your home and your father at the same time." She thought of the sadness and hardships the young Gabe Marcos must have endured.

Gabe's reflections seemed to transcend time, and he spoke in a low, hypnotic tone. "I was fourteen, and I remember it as if it were yesterday. Papá had been depressed for days. The stress of what was happening was just too much for him. Mamá finally persuaded him to come and eat supper.

"He stood at the head of the table for a minute, then made a strange gasping sound and fell to the floor. He died there before our eyes. His unrelenting drive killed him as surely as if a knife had been plunged into his heart. My mother and Anaya were hysterical. That day I became a man . . ."

The agonizing words chilled Krystal. She gasped with the impact of the acknowledgment, as did Gabe. Obviously he had not intended to say it. His fierce blue eyes were shimmering pools of intense sadness that had been kept bottled up in that masculine shell for twenty-one years.

"My God, Krystal—I've never told anyone that." He seemed to choke. His tone was hollow and lifeless.

The next thing Krystal knew she was cradling his head against her breasts. Tenderly she clutched him to her while her tears fell on his ebony hair. His arms wrapped fiercely around her, clinging desperately to her sudden strength.

They stayed that way, locked in time and emotion, the wind whipping around them, binding them together as did their clinging and crying and shared feelings. Finally

Krystal murmured, "Gabe, Gabe, I'm so sorry. What a heavy burden for a boy to carry—and a man to hide—all these years."

Finally he shifted from their tight embrace. He spoke, hesitantly at first. "Heart attack, they said later. But it was like he refused to live once the land was taken away. He had fought and worked—worked himself to death for something he couldn't have. It was futile. He was a defeated man, humiliated before his family, a failure to the memory of his ancestors. The years that he worked the hardest were for nothing when he lost it all."

"How difficult it must have been for your family—for you."

"I vowed then to vindicate my father, to restore what was rightfully his—to return respect to the Marcos name."

"Oh, Gabe, you have. You're known and respected throughout the state."

His blue eyes tore into her. "The debt is not fully paid, Krystal."

And she knew he meant her land. The words hurt her deeply and left her feeling absolutely helpless. She and Gabe were bound together, and yet they weren't. They shared similar pains; still the differences were great. They were again separate individuals, each carrying a separate burden. There had been a brief sharing. But each had a burden never to be shed completely.

Again Meg's haunting words returned to Krystal. "Strong attachment to the land, love of the earth" . . . oh, dear God . . . "a man who sells his land sells his mother!"

Eventually they began to walk around, talking occasionally. Gabe's face held a strange expression, as if he wanted to absorb the essence of the land around them into his very soul. He loved it, longed for it—and yet he didn't.

At last, as the winter sun began to set at the far western edge of their world, Gabe turned to her. "Ready to go?"

"Are you?"

He nodded and led the way back to the Bronco.

Krystal followed silently, feeling very much like she had been given a brief insight into the mysterious Gabe Marcos's innermost secrets. And indeed she had.

They rode away in silence. Leaving was a relief, although neither admitted it. After the things they had shared, what more could be said?

An hour later Gabe halted the vehicle in front of her adobe cottage, the last place they had made love. Now what had made her think of that? Krystal reflected sadly that it had been the last time they would ever make love. It was with a heavy heart that she came to that realization.

"Thank you, Gabe, for taking me today." Then she wondered why she had thanked him. He had set in motion the beginning of the end.

Gabe's voice was somber. "Maybe now you can see why I have always wanted this land back, Krystal. The place holds my past, my heritage. It means so much to me . . ."

"Yes, I can see that," she admitted, a strange quiet settling over her. "Would you like to come in for a cup of coffee? Or perhaps something stronger?"

"No, thank you, I have to get back to Starfire. We were gone longer than I had intended."

"Okay." Krystal swallowed hard. "Good-bye, Gabe." And she meant it. A huge knot in her throat threatened to choke off the normal air flow as she slipped quickly from the Bronco.

Krystal knew what she had to do, and she would waste no time doing it.

CHAPTER TEN

Two boxes were packed and another lay open on the table when the phone rang.

"Krystal, I got your message. What gives? Are you crazy?"

"Hmmm, some people probably think so," she quipped.

"Damnit Krystal, you know what I mean!" There was a no-nonsense quality to his tone.

"Take it easy, Jason," she answered, bracing herself for what she knew would be his inquisitive response. "I'm very sane. And realistic at last. Gabe Marcos will never give in. Never."

"Then we'll look for other sources. You suggested it yourself. Something else will turn up. It's just a matter of time, Krystal."

"There is no more time, Jason. I've changed my mind. I'm tired of fighting to stay. Sell it to Gabe."

He sighed with obvious exasperation. "I'll never understand you, Krystal. You know, before your visit here, I would have been delighted to receive this message. My first thought would have been that we could make a killing on this property. But now, after seeing you, hearing you talk about the High Valley Ranch and knowing how much it means to you, I think this sudden decision is a mistake."

"Wow, talk about your complete turnaround! I can't believe it's you, Jason! No, my mistake was in thinking I could make it up here. This is not where I belong. I see it clearly now."

"Krystal, hon, this is such a switch for you. You have always been so adamant about staying there. And I honestly think the ranch is good for you."

"Well, I've changed, Jason," she responded shortly. "I've changed my mind about what I want. I'll go to Santa Fe, open a shop there. Forget about these grand plans for a health spa."

"But, Krystal, I think I've found a financial backer for you. He wants to meet you. He would act as a silent partner and can supply any amount of money you need, believe me."

"Thank you, no. I'm ready to leave here."

"Krystal," he persisted. "Does it have anything to do with Gabe Marcos? With your relationship with him?"

"It has everything to do with him," she admitted. "I know him quite well now, Jason. Meg was right. He's old-generation Basque through and through. I'm sure he'll never change his mind. And I don't want to live up here so close to him. We'd do nothing but create misery for each other."

She knew in her heart that she couldn't stand seeing Gabe, even occasionally. Even if by some miracle he did come around to her way of thinking someday, she could never work with him. Her emotional attachment to the man was too great. It would tear her apart to see him and not be the one in his arms.

"Are you in love with the man?" Jason was never one to skirt the issue at hand.

She could be honest with him now. "Yes." He knew her well, even though he claimed not to be able to understand her.

"Damn, Krystal! How could you let that happen?" he exploded angrily.

She sighed at his typical male reaction, as if she could guide her emotions. "Sorry, Jason. It was something beyond my control. But leaving High Valley isn't. Please sell it for me. Then get busy on finding something for me in Santa Fe. Quick. I'm packing now."

"Krystal—"

She interrupted firmly. "I'm making only one stipulation to the sale—that Vegas Santee be offered the opportunity to continue to work here if he so desires. I want that option clause inserted for him."

"Okay, hon. It's as good as done."

"Thank you, Jason."

Krystal cradled the phone with a strange sense of relief. There, now. The loyal Vegas was taken care of, and she felt good about that. Jason could negotiate to his heart's content. No matter what he said, she knew he would love every minute of the selling process. And he would make sure she made a profit, she was confident. Right now she honestly didn't care about that. She just wanted to be free. Free of Gabe Marcos.

Most important, Gabe Marcos should be ecstatic. This was what he had wanted for twenty-one years. It was what he had fought for these past ten years. Now he could once again be in possession of the land of his ancestors—his roots. His father would be fully vindicated. And he would be free of her.

She bit her lip. What about Krystal North? Oh, she would be okay. Starting anew in Santa Fe wouldn't be so bad. Once again she would begin a new life. However, this time there would be no involvements. No entangling relationships. No husband, no Margo, no Gabe. Only Jason and Meg could be trusted, anyway. She took a deep, determined breath.

She would make it this time. After all, she wasn't easily broken. She wasn't crystal-thin and delicate—and she wasn't nearly as fragile as her name implied. She was shatter-proof. And she would prove it. Huge tears filled her emerald eyes as she grabbed the last of the stemware on the shelf and stuffed newspaper into its dainty bowl.

"Krystal, what the hell is the meaning of this?"

He stood, his feet apart, his arms akimbo, in the doorway of her bedroom. She tried not to meet those piercing blue eyes. She did not want to face the obvious questions there. Or the man!

"Don't you know how to knock? Or do you always intrude into a woman's bedroom whenever you please?" She folded a blue sweater neatly into the suitcase that lay open on her bed.

He gestured. "I knocked. Apparently you didn't hear me. I just got a call from my lawyer. What in the hell are you doing?"

Without looking up, she answered caustically, "This is called packing. It's what one does when one is moving." She was purposely sarcastic—it was the only way she knew to keep from crying, from screaming at Gabe Marcos. Damn him, anyway!

"Moving?" His tone matched hers. "Why don't you call it what it really is? You're running away again—escaping from something you don't want to face."

"I'm starting a new life. In Santa Fe. Since it was your idea, you should be extremely happy."

He folded his arms across the breadth of his chest and leaned against the door frame. "No, it doesn't make me extremely happy, Krystal. Why don't you stay and fight this thing out?" The challenge was obvious, but she wouldn't accept it. The fight in her was gone.

Krystal chuckled sardonically. "There is a line in 'The Gambler,' an old Kenny Rogers tune, that goes, 'You've got to know when to fold 'em.' Well, I gambled and I lost, and I sure as hell know when to fold 'em."

She didn't look up but continued unloading sweaters from the middle dresser drawer and methodically placing them in the suitcase. "I know when I'm defeated. There is no way I can compete with your love of this land, Gabe. So I'm letting you have it all back. And you will be rid of me and every obstacle that has ever stood in the way of your owning this land again. That should please you."

"Krystal, if you go, how will I get rid of this aching inside?"

She glanced up quickly, caught his piercing eyes, then turned away. She shoved the drawer closed with her knee and grasped the top one fiercely. "You'll have what you want!"

"Damnit, Krystal, I don't want anything but you!"

His large hands gripped her forearms with such ferocity, she dropped the handful of lace panties she held. "Gabe, please—"

"Krystal, I can't let you go! I won't! Can't you see that I'm tormented by you? I can't get you out of my mind!"

She looked at him defiantly, past the tight lips and tanned cheeks to those mesmerizing blue eyes. Would she be able to resist their power? "It will be so much easier to forget me when I'm not here."

"But I don't want to forget you. I want you here. With me," he insisted.

Through clenched teeth she muttered, "Well, you can't

have everything you want. Please let me go, Gabe. You're hurting my arms."

His long fingers loosened their grip. "I—I'm sorry, Krystal. I just—can't stand the thought of you leaving."

"Perhaps you don't understand, Gabe. It's either the land or me. Obviously you can't have both. It seems to me you've made that perfectly clear. Well, I'm through fighting. Knowing what I do about how much this land means to you, I realize there's no way you're going to let up. And you shouldn't. I'll admit, you deserve to have it. And, well, I just don't want to hang around here anymore. I'm perfectly willing to sell. It's simply a matter of drawing up the papers."

"*Querida,* I don't want it."

"I really don't give a damn about the selling price. I just want my equity out of it. I won't hold you over a barrel for a demanding amount. I just want out—what?"

"Didn't you hear me, Krystal? I don't want the damn land. I only want you."

"Perhaps you didn't hear me, Gabe Marcos. I'm not available anymore."

"What? There isn't another man—" His eyes flashed.

"A man? Hardly! I learn my lessons the hard way! But I learn! No one else is going to be involved in my life! I'm on my own this time. All alone! And unavailable!" She stooped to pick up the scattered panties.

Before she could reach for another lacy item, Gabe's strong hands lifted her against him, his lips claiming hers. Breathlessly she clung to his shoulders as she attempted to regain control of her senses. One touch and she was again swirling into the warm magic of Gabe Marcos! But she had to put a stop to this! She had to!

He held her securely, closely, and moved just enough to

speak. "Don't you understand what I'm saying, Krystal? I love you . . ."

It was the first time he had ever said that, and she felt a wild stab inside. Her head swam dizzily, and she leaned against him for support while she regained her composure.

"Gabe, I—I can't keep fighting you like this. It's too painful."

"Then don't fight it, Krystal. Give in to our love."

"I—I have given in too much. I can't do it again."

"Why?" He gave her a slight shake.

"Because I'm too emotionally involved. I can't turn my love on and off that easily."

"I don't want it turned off, *querida,* ever." He molded her firmly to him.

"I don't understand, Gabe," she protested, knowing she couldn't resist him if he didn't let go soon. She was far too weak. "I'm giving you what you want. The land will be yours. Please don't make any more demands of me."

"I don't care about the land anymore. I just want you, Krystal. I love you more than anything!"

Did she hear him correctly? "Gabe, you're not making any sense. I know why you took me out there and why you feel the way you do. I understand, and it's okay. Perhaps we can still see each other in Santa Fe."

What was she saying? Did she want to prolong this agony? No, she just didn't want to lose Gabe completely. In that instant Krystal knew she loved him deeply, loved him more than she had ever loved anyone. She would give up anything to make him happy, including what she needed most.

"No, Krystal. It's not okay. I—I was wrong all those years. After our visit to the old homestead, I realized that the memory of it had been glorified by my imagination.

The place held as many bad reminders as good. And no matter what the attachment to the land, it's still a tangible, material thing. Compared to the value of your love, it's nothing."

"N-nothing?" Krystal stammered, recalling him telling her of his twenty-one years of struggle and hard work and desire for that land—of unfulfilled familial destiny—of vindication for the Marcos name. Of heart and soul in the land. "Gabe, I know how important this is to you. I want you to accomplish what you've worked for so long—to fulfill your father's dream."

"I don't want anything without you, *mi amor.*"

"I'm sorry, Gabe. My price is too high. I want love and a commitment."

"You mean marriage?" There was a half-smile on his lips.

"Yes." She nodded. "I can't banter my feelings around like this anymore. My doubts—"

"If it's marriage you want, *querida,* then it's marriage we'll have!"

"Gabe!" She leaned weakly against him. "Do you mean it?"

"I love you, Krystal. More than anything in this world—including that miserable bit of rocky earth out there. I want you with me—as my wife."

"Oh, Gabe, I can't believe what I'm hearing! Maybe I love you and want you so much that I'm dreaming—"

"This is no dream, *mi amor* . . ." His fierce kiss closed off his words, sealing his admission of love and dispelling any notion that she was dreaming. Emotions were real and passions high as Krystal clung to Gabe, and they made love in the little adobe house in High Valley.

* * *

"Gabe? Gabe! Are you awake? I think it's snowing again. Listen." Krystal's spirited voice broke the peaceful silence of their cabin retreat.

"Hmmm? You can't hear snow, Krystal."

"Well, I hear something out there, and I'll bet it's snow!"

"Good guess. Maybe we'll be snowed in for the entire week. But it's probably just the wind." He nuzzled her earlobe, which persisted in hiding behind her tousled blond strands.

"But, Gabe," she insisted, giggling as he tickled her neck with soft nibbles. "Today is our wedding day. We've already had our blood tests and everything!"

"It'll save. The important things last . . ." He pulled her closer.

"Important? This is the most important day of my life, Gabe Marcos!" Krystal sat up and pulled the colorful Indian blanket modestly in front of her breasts. "Gabe, wake up! This is the day I'm supposed to become Mrs. Gabriel Marcos! Oh, damn! It's snowing again! I just know it!" she wailed.

He hooked an arm around her bare torso, his hand grasping the silken skin on her hip. "Come here, *querida*. We'll talk about it."

"I don't want to talk about it. What are we going to do about more snow?"

"Good for business . . ." he mumbled from the pillow.

"Just look," she exclaimed and bounded from the bed, her bare buttocks shining. Drawing the drapes, Krystal stared out at the silver-white landscape. New snow fell on the redwood deck and the empty hot tub. Damn! They couldn't even enjoy the tub! "Oh, Gabe, can't you *do* something?" She stamped her foot in frustration, and to get his attention.

He grinned at her, his hands folded under his head. "Krystal, *querida,* I had nothing to do with this. I'm snowed in, too, remember. But *I* happen to like it here." He smiled admiringly at her nude figure glinting in the daylight. "I must say, the snow-covered mountain landscape is gorgeous! I love the blond nude in the foreground. Now why don't you come on back in here with me, where it's warm."

Her fists on her hips, Krystal stared outside again, then decided the cozy bed was too inviting to resist. With a delighted squeal she dove in, parting the covers and falling gratefully into Gabe's welcoming arms.

"Get back in here where you belong, woman. Marriage vows or not, you're mine. And I'm yours. You know that. Surely a day or two more won't matter."

"No, not really." She sighed. "I just had my heart set on being your wife today. I love you so, Gabe . . ." She raked her fingers sensuously through his dark hair and pulled his face around so she could kiss him.

"Hmmm, I love you, too," he murmured, nestling her against his chest. "Ah, I fought it, I'll admit. I was drawn to you from the first. But that was something short of love. With your blond hair and those bewitching green eyes—oh, how I wanted you!"

Krystal nodded, pressing her lips to his warm, softly pounding chest. "I've never done anything like that before, Gabe. I was caught up in the holiday spirit that evening, and the man involved. Afterward I felt ashamed of myself. Plus I just knew I had ruined my chances of ever working out a deal with you."

"Your little proposal for a merger threw me for a loop,

all right! But I think we have worked out the best business deal possible. We'll just keep it all in the family! However, you are definitely in charge of the spa and exercise programs. I'll have nothing to do with it!"

"Do you mean that you still want to build the spa?" Krystal asked delightedly.

"Of course! The whole works! That land is perfect for a health spa!"

"Why you—" she sputtered. "Why didn't you tell me before rather than trying to discourage me?"

He laughed wickedly. "And admit I was wrong? I was never man enough to admit that—until now."

"Truthfully, Gabe, did you ever seriously consider a merger?" She tugged playfully on his earlobe.

"Never! Oh, you presented some good arguments. I knew I needed that road through the valley. Desperately! And you knew the spa wouldn't detract from Starfire's business. It will add to it, as you said. However, I was driven toward one blind dream, and that was to repossess that land. It wasn't because I wanted or needed it but because it was part of my heritage. I thought I had to have it again. Until I saw it."

"Gabe, when did you change your mind? And why?"

"Oh, after the trip back to the homestead. I suppose it came about as an evolution of my feelings. After spending Christmas with you I knew I was falling in love with those lovely green eyes of yours, as well as the rest of you. Then, when you told me about Margo, I knew that even though our reasons were different, you were equally driven to own that property. Both those things scared hell out of me. So I bailed out for a few days. Went to Santa Fe with Anaya."

"Did you tell her?"

"I didn't have to. She knew I was in love. And miserable."

Krystal was curious about this sister she had never met. "Did she give you sisterly advice?"

"God, no!" Gabe chuckled. "She just said, 'Love always complicates things.' Then she left me to work it out myself. My solution was to take you with me back to the homestead. I thought that would convince you how much I needed that property."

"Oh, it did. I knew I had lost the battle. And I gave up the entire war. Even if you changed your mind about the merger, I couldn't bear working with you on anything else. I love you too much to see you and not hold you."

His hand stroked her face lovingly. "You know, it's funny. That trip back home changed my distorted memory of all these years. Going there was like a form of exorcism. I looked around the place and realized that there were as many unhappy memories there as happy ones. And suddenly it all meant nothing to me if I couldn't have you. You are everything to me, Krystal—*mi joyalita navidad*—my little Christmas jewel—I love you."

"You make me feel so special, Gabe. I'll always cherish my memories of this first Christmas we spent together. It was my best Christmas—ever."

"Next year will be better, *mi amor.* We'll be together as a family, creating our own heritage."

"When will we get started on this ambitious project?"

He grinned. "When it stops snowing. But don't worry. I'll get you to the church today if I have to use a snowmobile."

"That's probably the only way we can make it down that horrible mountain road of yours!"

"Ours, *mi amor.* Look, Krystal, it's stopped snowing," he whispered.

"Wonderful! Now we can get out of here and start making our own little family history!"

"I'd rather make love," he teased, cupping a breast possessively. "You know how I feel about making love in the morning. It's so refreshing!"

"Gabe . . ." She pressed her slender, cream-colored body to his tanned, hard muscles. His passion enflamed boldly against her. Yes, he was hers, and it was a happy, wonderful, giddy feeling. "Don't forget about our wedding . . . oh, Gabe!"

"Later, *querida,* later," he murmured between kisses. "I promise that by tonight you will be Mrs. Gabe Marcos." He settled his frame over her, asserting his loving force against her receptive softness. "Maybe we'll be snowed in again . . ."

"I'd like that," she purred, succumbing to his magic and the silver enchantment that enshrouds all lovers in the mysterious Sangre de Cristos.